Maddalena Battello
Eligio Linoci

Light Love

Novel

Impossible loves never end

*True love is when the heart beats faster than
the mind may think*

The law.

To those who always smile despite everything

How does a woman feel after bariatric surgery?

This is a question that only those who have passed can answer. Overcome all the obstacles pre and post-operative, after about a year from the intervention, you begin to savor a scent of new life, I would say sparkling. No one believes it at first, when they tell you that you will be another person, because deep down it seems impossible that physical change also leads to a mental change. Instead, it is just like that, the 40 or 50 kilos lost in a couple of years are nothing compared to what happens from an emotional point of view.

Suddenly you feel powerful, capable, unlimited, as if until then your life had been static and now had to take off.

It's not easy to manage this new state of mind, or at least it wasn't easy for me.

Combining work, family, sports, leisure is no longer a problem, energy and vitality become a constant, sometimes to the detriment of those close to you. The scenario is this, a halved body, an electrified mind, and an exaggerated desire for redemption.

Those who live in obesity only when they lose weight realize what their suffering has been. For some it is precisely being stigmatized, for others the inability to perform simple actions, for others still not being able to stop. I honestly don't know what band I belong to, the only thing I can say for sure is that I don't want to be who I was anymore. We often felt invisible, unwanted, locked in a shell of fat that on the one hand protected us but on the other isolated us.

*Surely now none of us is like that anymore.
The desire to experiment, to open up to a new
world, to be noticed, to cultivate passions, to
satisfy one's ego and to live life to the full and
not just survive is stronger.*

*Personally, I do not like to compare the photos
of the before and after, because it hurts me to
see how I have mistreated my body, also for
this reason I prefer to meet new people who do
not have a term of comparison. Surely someone
will think that I have gone crazy or that I have
the famous midlife crisis, I just believe that I
am selfishly chasing that life that
had gotten out of hand.*

*Writing this novel together with Eligio, also a
bariatric patient, was a great opportunity for
personal growth. The demonstration that even
we "invisible bulky" have something to tell,
dreams to realize, and above all a vitality yet to
be discovered.*
*This story is about a woman who seeks
lightness, in love and in everyday life, the result
of fantasies, lived experiences and sleepless
nights, will remain for us an irrepressible
sharing of emotions.*

Prologue

I find myself here, in this bar in front of the station. To drink my coffee. I'm thinking about you intensely, I have chills all along my body. I think about the desires I had. As much as I wanted you, Sought. My life has been that of a woman who wanted her own dimension, who always wanted what she dreamed of.

It is said that dreams come true, but I don't really know if mine will ever come true. I have a notebook in front of me, and a blue biro pen. I would have preferred it black because the black stroke gives more prominence to the notes.

I want to write down all the bad moments of my life and then erase them with a definitively decided trait.

How much I wanted you, how much I wanted those hugs that I have always missed. My life has passed like a steam train, I live with the desire to meet you sooner or later, to hold you and hug you.

Perhaps this dream will come true one day. In this bar I watch a couple touching their hands, looking at each other with eyes in love, if I will ever be able to experience the same sensations. This life of sacrifices, of nights spent thinking about what it would have been if one day I had managed to free myself from this burden that I have always carried inside.

This does not look at me freely, as I wanted. The days passed inexorably fast, without respite, I wanted to get to you. I left behind a lifetime to discover new opportunities.

I wanted to get out of a shell that couldn't hatch. A burden that made me hide, but at the same time, told me that I would make it sooner or later, that I would be able to escape.
And suddenly the lightness of things came.

A feather that wrapped me, took me, and made me fly. Here I am, it is me, with the fullness of life that I have in my body and the awareness of being able to cry out to the world that there are.

Then my heart also began to be light. To take flight, as he had never done before. To feel the emotions that I repressed, that I suffocated. I came out of this body that did not belong to me. I found my anchor, my foothold to hold on to, to bind myself to. I discovered love that perhaps I had never felt or felt before.

My heart started beating again, strong, as if it wanted to explode. Now it is active, I want to start living again, if I had done it before. I want to be me, I owe it to my daughter Cecìle, to her who has always seen an unsuitable mother. I want to be everything to myself, to someone who loves me and who accepts what I have become.

I want to be a feather, white, beautiful and above all light. The weight I have always had on me, in my mind, in my heart, I want it to no longer be part of me. I want to be that feather that she loves lightly, that wants to fly, that never stops, in front of any obstacle, that continues, driven by the wind, its race until it reaches another heart that will give her love. You have arrived, light love that makes me live, that makes me emotional. How beautiful life is when you discover that you love and are loved. When you run towards a new future, full of emotions.

It is precisely that I was looking for. And, perhaps, I touch it with my hand. Light Love

Montpellier, 13 March 2013

Hello love. I am here, in front of my black coffee, on the boat that takes me to that wonderful view of the sea. There is a sea breeze that runs through my body. I feel chills, perhaps because I write to you, and every time, wherever I do, I have emotions that upset me from head to toe. This coffee has an authentic flavor, as authentic is the great desire to have you here with me. The dawn emanates beautiful colors that are part of me, they are my essence.
The great magic of the sun rising from the sea. Our sea. For some time, I thought of writing to you, but many times I thought about it. I didn't make it; many fears grip me. I wanted to write to you to tell you about me, who I was and what I have become. I desperately searched through my drawers for a picture of me from when I was a child and teenager. I have not found any, maybe I will have thrown them all away. I always liked myself, I saw myself beautiful. Now I look in the mirror and I don't know if I see the same woman. I would like to tell you about when I went to the Mercato des Halles Laillac.
Those scents, the fruit, the spices.

The colors of love that I would like to live with you, but that I have often seen fade. Living like this is consuming me. I went through joys but also many sorrows. Now I have the awareness that I want to change. To wear other robes.

To color my days and to shout to the world my freedom.

I imagine you sitting by the river, waiting for me. You don't know how much I looked for you, how much I wanted you. In these years I dreamed of a great love that would lead me towards the salvation so much sought.

When I run towards the horizon, I don't know what I'm going to encounter, but I know that what I want is already looking for me. Your hands, your mouth, your smile, the one that will make me happy forever. I look for a simple love that knows how to make me fly high, beyond the clouds, above that blanket of beliefs, often taken for granted, that make me feel inadequate, sometimes useless. This is what I would like from you. Light love.

Your Coraline

"The soul of an individual resides in the books he reads and would like to write"

Sometimes while I'm walking around, I like to walk into the bookstore. Taking a book and flipping through a few pages, relaxes me. I identify myself; I imagine how what was written in those first pages could reflect in my life. This made me dream and I was happy and serene with myself.

I always wanted to write a book, about my life, about my passions. So maybe I would have understood what was wrong in these days spent chasing who knows what, who knows who. This great desire may have been passed down to me by my father even though I don't even remember who he was.

He left home when I was 13 years old.
A tall and big man who sometimes even frightened because of his size.

I think he has loved me since I was born, a
special affection of a man who was never
present. At least that's what my mom tells
me. Those few times we were able to talk
about him, he pointed me to a man
dedicated to work, always around and
with typically Nordic characteristics.

My father was from the north, he was
born in Husavik, a small town in Iceland,
a very cold, almost polar place.
This coldness, after all, has also been
transmitted to the family.
With my mother there was never much
agreement.
As a typical Parisian, she did not like her
closed ways very much, she was not a
docile character.
They met in Paris, my father worked at the
Icelandic Consulate in France, in
Versailles. From there they soon moved to
Montpellier, in the south of France,
precisely to Juvignac.

It was a difficult childhood for me. I
suffered the unhealthy relationships of my
parents who quarreled all the time.
This has always created discomfort, bad
mood. I barely remember happy moments.
My mother was also a woman with the
habit of drinking, which left indelible
memories in me. Maybe my father didn't
have all the wrongs to leave home, she
didn't even have an easy character.

My father at the Consulate was in charge
of the State Library of Reykjavik, which
had offices all over Europe, so I think he
transmitted to me the desire for the book.

He traveled a lot.
He was passionate, he read books in large
quantities, a cultured man, so he probably
did not bond with my mother's basic
education. It was his dream to write one
and he did it: he wrote a novel about two
elders and their love story. I remember
that my mother told me about it, and
although there was no positive epilogue in
their marriage, she told me about it with

great enthusiasm. This story written by my father left in me a thought, a desire: to live a love story in old age.

He had put so much ardor, so much feeling into it. It was the great love of the protagonists, which made the story itself interesting.

This is the memory of my father, of his book, of the kindness lavished. Despite his character, in the lines of that novel, there was passion.

Inspired by his words, I discovered the love to be sought, the almost eternal love, the love that is good for the heart. I began to treat him, although I did not know what to expect. My mother taught me to love everything. She always said that if I found a man it would be a gift. I was not so convinced of this, because I always believed that I would be the one to give and transmit love. And if I had found the man who would have understood it, perhaps, I would have achieved my goal. I spent my adolescence in Montpellier, where I went to school, attended a riding course and an oratory of Benedictine monks.
This last frequentation, I think, did not benefit me so much, because after all I was already a rebellious spirit, a woman leaning towards escape.

I didn't see myself standing on a straw
chair learning prayers and oracles.

Horse riding taught me elegance and
horse education as a way of life.
A troubled adolescence, lived between
bridging the absence of a father, and
enduring a mother who increasingly sinks
into alcohol dependence. In me was born
the need to run away and cling to
something, to someone who would make
me happy. Yes, there was this spasmodic
request for happiness, which I missed so
much since I was a child. I had dolls,
games, clothes. But I needed something
else, something that I needed
it would have made the heartbeat. A gift I
received at Christmas, a new game, a new
dress, did not give me those emotions. I
realized that my heart was closed with a
big padlock inside a chest.
That was what I felt.

A casket that guarded all my suffering
that one day would be ready to fly away
and leave room for my light love.

"My father's common sense, and my mother's tongue, assist me"

Julianne and Orvar have a way, all their own, of being a couple. They practically do not coexist. They are always far from each other.

She is my mother, Julianne Cagnet, born in Paris, rooted in the capital French, and moved to Montpellier just for love. Although later it proved to be only a marginal aspect. Therefore, I never quite understood what it was. My mother was like that, she loved in her own way, as she wanted, as her head told her. He thought a lot about his things, his affections, the dog, and the cat from which he did not detach even a minute.

Very strong character, a true artist of who cares. In the truest sense of the word.

My mom is the first of three children, two girls and a boy. The smallest is Christof, the average Annabelle.

A quiet family, dedicated to the
production of hats, purely feminine. Those
that were used in the 60s/70s. Merchants
hatters, in short.

In Paris it was a trend to wear a hat, it has
always been an important and fashionable
accessory for a woman.

My mom was the hostess, she was the one
who kept everything under control.
The one who managed the family assets
was basically the owner of the house.
Because my grandmother had
disappeared very young, while my
grandfather a fallen in the war in the
Russian Campaign.

My father. A great man, Icelandic from Husavik. He had lived in Iceland until the age of 23, then moved to Paris, and there he met my mother.

I can't say if it was a great love, I can only say that I saw him attached to her. Feeling that was not repaid.

Evidently because she was very busy keeping the family going, being the adult who acted as the mother of all. But he was close to her, however he loved her.

Very often they slept in different houses, each on their own, because of my father's work and because my mother never had this sense of coexistence.

Even if one day they had a child, it would have been the same. And when you took this topic, the core of the speech was always that. Neither of them aspired to coexistence. Therefore, they saw each other a few times. When I was born, my dad was out on business in Germany.

He came back to see me in swaddling
clothes just 18 days later.

It must have been the Nordic mentality;
the fact is that I lived in an already
disunited environment.
My father, however, was a gentleman, as I
remember him. He was always
affectionate and kind to me, and not just
because I was his daughter.
He had never lived with a woman, and I
also think my mom was the only woman
in his life. He was a shy guy, reserved and
dedicated to his work.
I remember one evening at dinner at our
house, I was very small, we talked about
this, and this situation.
"Who then I do not understand what the
problem of coexistence is" my mother had
said
"Why be unhappy seven days a week if
we can be happy when we see each
other?"

I think the problem was my mom. Because she had always lived short relationships, of which she had immediately tired.

He would not have taken care to pamper them these loves.
She was a very free girl; you didn't have to contradict her. She always had to do what her head told her.

For her, obsession or possession were not characteristics that those who would love her had to have. Feeling the breath on her neck made her suffer, made her closed in a box.

She was a lioness, a conquering animal. It was she who had to have control over everything. Here, perhaps I understand, having always lived with her, from whom I inherited a certain way of doing, that strong and free character.

I don't know if it was positive, it happened
in my mind to think one thing but then I
did another just like she did.
With his actions he certainly conditioned
me and made me miss my father more and
more.

From him I took the confidentiality, the
acumen in doing things, the reflective
being on everything, although mortified
by the often-impetuous ways of my
mother.

That evening my father said to me: "With
a woman you must never give the idea of
being completely his, otherwise you are in
check."

 But his life went to slam against my
mother who held him in her hand.

Indifference was a brilliant idea for him, in
the family relationship. Being away for a
long time made him feel not his
possession.

My mother, to tell the truth, never
suffered from all this. On the contrary, she
was pleased, even though she was not
satisfied as a woman.

He always said he deserved another kind
of man. But I wondered: how would she
do if she wanted to be alone first of all?

But then he replied: "After all, a man is only good for fucking, and in any case, you are not the only one I want close." And here is the reply: "Do you realize? I have a line of women who would make false cards for me and the only one I want to be with answers me like this. Life is truly absurd." Life is absurd. These were the few evenings spent with mine. In those very rare times, they were with me.

"Presence doesn't always tell the truth, but absence just can't lie"

"Dad has not called? it has been ten days now that he does not mom tell me something"
 "Dad will not call for now. and will not even come back to visit us, at least for now." I didn't know what to think about that answer. If he had disappeared, if he had died.

All this distressed me, my mother seemed reluctant to give information. And I waited in vain every day for the phone to ring to hear his voice, as he had done in the past.

This time, I felt it, it was different. There must have been a quarrel that I was not aware of, which will have broken all plans. At least my father's. Because my mothers were definitely not to see him again, since she had never believed in this relationship.

Sometimes I wonder how they could
conceive, with what feeling?

From that moment I found myself without
a father, and I will always blame her.
I find this letter from my mother, one
morning. It's been five years since my
father left home, some lukewarm contact,
but nothing else.

Dear Coraline, it is the mother who writes to you. I think I should tell you a few things about your father, but I couldn't tell her in person. We never agreed, there had always been something that took us away. But we really wanted to have you, to have a child of our own. I confess that we could not, and, in the end, I decided to realize my dream by finding an alternative solution, which I never confessed to dad. Now that you are a woman, I wanted to reveal this secret to you. Maybe he was the problem, and you understand what problem I'm talking about. I wanted you at all costs and, although it is not the right thing I should have done, I succeeded.

Your father will never know because he would be too sick, so I ask forgiveness. Also, of the fact that I am writing it to you and not saying it verbally. Your mom...

I sat down and carefully read several
times. I wanted to understand the message
my mother wanted to convey to me. What
he wanted to tell me as well as ask me for
forgiveness. There are secrets that often
must remain so. I did not quite
understand what the alternative he was
talking about was, but the fact is that I did
not care. I was there, and I was the
daughter of both.

I didn't want to know anything else.
I would have hurt my father too by hiding
it now that I knew it.
But when would I tell him? Never.
He was far away, disappeared.
At least know where he was, what he did,
where he lived. Nothing.

This not to mention my parents was just a
way to protect me, to make me feel good
and see me happy. Although this was not
the happiness I sought and desired.

My life continued serenely. Without any
jolts. I followed my mother in this fight
against alcohol and, in the meantime, I
studied and wrote.

I put black and white on notes, many, I
filled whole notebooks. Notebooks that I
piled up in a drawer. I would have taken
them back, read and reread, as if they were
a personal diary.
Who knows if they will have a meaning,
or it will be just the outburst of a girl who
grew up too quickly? I was young, I
would have needed the carefreeness of
that age. I knew people, I talked to them.
I was a girl who, despite the family
vicissitudes, I managed to socialize and
make a life for myself. Now I needed a
love, someone by my side who was not
my mother, because I had a concept of
love of my own and I was not ready to
love. Someone had to teach me.

I wanted to live my youth with such
serenity. I didn't want to become like my
managers. There was this search for
escapism in me. Later I met a guy I
always saw passing in front of my house.
He was a tall, thin, cute guy. He would
pass by in a very large red car, slow down
when he was in front, and turn around to
look. I watched him from my window on
the ground floor and realized that he
smiled when he saw my gaze, then he
continued his run.

This for quite some time.
My mother told me she knew him. He was
the son of a couple who had recently
moved there. He came from the North of
France, from Rouen. He was an engineer,
recently graduated, and his father was a
member of the Army.

Their house was about a kilometer away
from ours and he walked that road every
morning and then returned in the evening
at dusk. But I saw him in the morning.

—

One Sunday afternoon I was watering the plants in the driveway in front of the house. I was behind and felt myself tapping my back. I turned around and it was him.
He apologized for the intrusion: "My name is Jean Philippe."

"Do you want to have a tea with me tonight?" And I, without even hesitating for a moment, said yes. Deep down we were just getting to know each other.
I didn't like it very much, to tell the truth, but I was intrigued by his direct way of inviting me out.
I loved studying the people I met, observing carefully and then taking notes on one of the many notebooks that I keep with jealousy.

He picked me up with his red car and took
me to a nearby place. We chatted for quite
a while, talking about so many things,
about me, about him, about his work,
about his family. Of my family I
remember having told little, I did not want
to reveal the problems I was experiencing,
it was not shame mine, but desire that the
dirty clothes remain within the walls of
the house.

I remember that evening we laughed a lot.
And it was a goal for me. After all, laughter,
smiles are good for the soul. And that night
I appreciated them very much. He drove
me home. There was no kiss, not even on
the cheek. You could see in him an innate
sense of decorum. Maybe I would have
even wanted a kiss, to smell his skin, but I
didn't look for it either.

I slept well that night because I felt
wanted, wanted, although I never knew if
it was infatuation or anything, I was
happy and that was the important thing.
The night flew by. And I may have even
dreamed, I don't remember it.

"My baby, do you have coffee with me?"
"Of course, wait for me to get off"
I slipped into his car, and we went to a
café to get some takeaway coffees. We
climbed a nearby hill and lay on the grass
watching the sunset, with our coffee still
in our hands. It was a special moment for
me, of those moments that you live with
great enthusiasm. Still, it was just a coffee.
But this time I was convinced that
something more would happen.
Calling me a treasure also meant a lot to
me.

We talked a lot about ourselves, our lives,
our affections, and how much each of us
felt the need to be together.

Well, maybe all this was the push that made me fall in love with him. I was not aesthetically attracted to it, but I loved the way to approach it, to open its heart and give it.

 Mine was dry, inappetent with a desire to savor sensations that would have made me fly. Now I felt it was time.

At my age and with the family situation I had, I had to give myself something that would awaken my heart. I remember spending a beautiful evening. On that lawn everything was more beautiful, more harmonious.

He was very shy and insecure, was that what I wanted? Maybe not. I would have liked a more vigorous man. But when he spoke, he caught me.

We kissed, for a long time. They were not
exciting kisses, but I felt within me the joy
of being desired. This made me feel good
and I left out other sides that I saw as
unsuitable for me. I wanted to live those
moments. And so, I did.

"I think I'm in love with you. From that
moment I saw you behind that window I
absolutely wanted to know you, to live
you."

I didn't think I was in love with him, but I
accepted his giving himself completely to
me.

We made love. It was not beautiful, not
very intense, but I still felt a man who
loved me. I gave myself to him, although I
was not fascinated, except by his voice and
his manners.

He was very sweet, having done it there,
under that starry sky, with the scent of
wildflowers around us was very engaging.

That evening spent among the absolute
beauty of nature gave a turning point to
my life.

Our relationship continued with ups and
downs, but all this because of me, I was
never satisfied. Maybe because I wasn't
used to it. He satisfied me in everything.
He wanted me with him.

Trying this experience that made me
forget what I went through in the family
for me was lifeblood.

But love is something else, at least that's how I've always thought.   Maybe I just wanted to experiment. After two years, we decided to get married. We did it quietly, with few guests. In a small rural church, it was October 6, I was 25 years old. I thought it was the right time and above all I wanted to escape from my usual routine. My mother agreed, after all it could not be otherwise, since she would always have wanted her life without anyone to turn around her. He agreed and was also happy.

"Coraline, you know how much I love you and I would like to see you always so serene. I will be by your side, at any time. I know I'm not the best mom in the world but know that now is your time. To detach yourself to love and do what you want."

I don't know if he really told me or if he wanted me to get married to leave home and make his life more free from hangings.
I laughed at those statements, they seemed to me to be said in a joking tone.

But she was my mother, and I had to believe her. After all, he was my only point of reference, despite his character and his unavailability.

Too bad for my father who was not there. That he was gone. Paternal support would have been of great help to me. A close father is always an outstretched hand.

My mother did not move a finger to look for him, who knows in what corner of the world he had hidden.

This saddened me, but I had to think about myself, about what I was doing. I knew it would be an important step. I was a little afraid it was too early. After all, we didn't know each other enough, and it wasn't even a love at first sight.

I loved him and I wanted to build something with him, that's what interested me. After all, my satisfaction would have been to form a family of my own, after my childhood I had dedicated it to thinking about my mother and little about me.

Now I was the leading actress of my life, marriage would give me that sense of inner security I was looking for.

But was I really sure? At this point I don't know either. A marriage is an important step, and you do it with the person you love.

And I still didn't feel in love with this man, although he gave me a very strong sense of stability. But there was no love, and that made me restless, unsure of what I was going to do.

Meanwhile we get married!
It was afternoon, I arrived in this little church with my beautiful white dress. I would have preferred it colorful, because of my strange whimsical ideas that I have always had.

I entered accompanied by my mother. She was moved, and this emotion of hers gave me anxiety, as if to want to go back and not pierce the entrance of the church.

A boy sang the wedding march. There were few guests, they must have been perhaps a dozen. Just the close relatives and a friend of Jean Philippe, who would have been our witness together with the sister of the promised
On my side only a brother of my mother came from Paris. Separated, with two children never met.
In fact, I had never even met his ex-wife. My mom had excluded the rest of her family. This was her.
Jean was dressed as a little Lord. Very elegant, facilitated by a slender and thin physique, compared to me who suffered for a few extra pounds, but who did not yet put me in difficulty. But I didn't feel very comfortable. The party to follow was just a refreshment.
We would soon leave for a short weekend in Lisbon, a city I particularly loved.
I had taken my step. I still can't say now if I was wrong or done it right.
I certainly wanted to detach myself from my mother, and that was already a decisive step for me. And I did.

"I never thought that conceiving a child would be such a great emotion."

After some time, when I woke up on a cold March morning, I had a strange feeling. I sat down and thought a lot, I didn't believe it, I was pregnant. It seemed impossible to me that I would be able to become a mother.

Actually, it scared me, I was speechless. I didn't see it with negativity, in fact perhaps it was my only unexpected joy, although I didn't feel ready.

In the meantime, I had begun to go on a diet, because I noticed that my weight was increasing more and more, also conditioned by stress. I didn't work, I had a lot of time available, I walked, but with little enthusiasm. I got tired right away. My body was weak.

I stopped to think how I could tell Jean. I waited for him to come back. I was anxious, he looked at me a little worried because my face was tried. I couldn't easily hide my feelings.

"What is Coraline? Don't feel well? Will it not be the fault of the diet you are doing? That then, two months have already passed, and I see you increasing more and more."

It was these words that punched me in the stomach. I had never seen him so harsh towards me. Where had the Jean I had known gone? Sweet, caring. Where?

I was surprised by this lack of tact. Was he right? But also no. It didn't seem like the way to talk to the woman you say you love.

I made him dinner and sat next to him and watched him.

"What do you look at? What's wrong? Today was a difficult day at work, excuse me if I turned to you like that. However, you should be more careful not to gain weight."

He infuriated even more by justifying with the fact that he had spent a difficult day at work.
And I? What did I mean? A woman who always had to cancel herself. That he had to suffer his moods? I wanted to give him such good news, so important, but I went to bed early and tired as I was, I collapsed.

When he came to bed I expected an apology, but it wasn't. And I, I didn't tell him anything.
I kept this secret for about a month, when one day I felt sick, fainted, and took me to the hospital. In visiting me, the doctor on call could only note the current situation.

When he announced that I was at least eight weeks pregnant, he looked at me and said nothing.

A bitter quarrel ensued. He was just about making me weigh him down, rather than hugging me and telling me he was happy.

They were moments that made me think of running away. I no longer had Jean Philippe whom I had known. It was another person.
I spent the first six months with a pregnancy that fortunately proceeded well, but I did everything myself.

For the umpteenth time he did not seem happy, and it made me feel bad. As if I had committed who knows what crime in becoming a mother.

I felt inadequate, suddenly unloved, not wanted as before. The weight kept rising, because of my belly that welcomed a beautiful little girl.

A couple of months before giving birth I felt him a little closer, even though I had already acquired the awareness of knowing how to manage myself, as I had always done in my life and also in my family.

My baby is born just before Christmas.
Very beautiful and chubby, she all looks like my father. At that moment I saw him in front of my eyes, and I realized how much I missed him, especially now that I needed
a strong figure, the one that Jean was not able to be.

Now I understand many things, I connect my childhood with my being unsuitable.
But now I felt stronger, with so much energy, and happy to have a daughter.

"What do we call it?" he told me.
"You have any ideas? We have never
talked about it until now. You didn't seem
to care"
"Choose yourself since you carried out this
pregnancy alone. I agree with everything."

This passivity had just diminished him,
made him become a man without balls,
sometimes childish. I had married a child.

My anxieties grew, about how I would
deal with my new status as a mother and
probably also a father.

I called her Cecìle. A beautiful name,
which in English is abbreviated to Sissy. It
means blind, invisible. My daughter was
invisible to everyone except me. I carried
her in my womb for nine months, alone,
with a father who was totally disinterested
as if it were not his.

I am proud of myself, for my strength and my constancy, even my mother seemed changed, you could read pride in her eyes, as if for once she considered me a woman.

Cecìle is a smiling, lively child. This was important to me, the rest I would have faced, as always with the heart.

*"Friendship is certainly the best balm for
the wounds of a disappointed love"*

Cecìle grew every day, I did it too but of
weight. The relationship with Jean also
became heavier and heavier. He was no
longer what he was before. He was out on
business all the time. In this I was
reminded of the specter of the life I lived
with my father who was always absent. I
didn't feel comfortable, mine was a cage
from which I would hardly be able to get
out unscathed.

But now I had my daughter to look after
and raise.
Meanwhile, I had met a neighbor, blonde,
in her forties with whom I spent a lot of
time.

She had two children, little more than
teenagers, and an ex-husband. He had left
her for a much younger girl, whom he met
in the office where he worked.

She was a beautiful woman, very jovial,
she understood my problems very well,
because for her it was a dejà vu. Her name
was Annette, and at the time she saw
herself with a man older than her, who
made her happy. At least that's what he
said, even if they saw very little because of
his work commitments. I loved his
friendship the support he offered me
almost daily.

She was of Italian origin like him, who
very often went to Italy for work, while
she stayed at home alone with the boys.
He worked occasionally in the morning,
and in the afternoon, he dedicated himself
to doing after-school work for some
students.

Hers was a story like many, she became pregnant young, before the wedding she had married forced by events, she was certainly not in love.

She didn't even treat her well, she stayed with him only for her son, and because she wouldn't know where to go.
His story had intrigued me a lot, like the relationship with this new companion. It was an important confrontation for me to understand what was wrong with my marriage and why Jean had changed like this.

Sometimes I also thought he had another woman, maybe a work colleague. But then I told myself that it would be impossible since he was reserved and shy and hardly able to fall in love with another person.

But was ours true love? Certainly not,
absolutely. I never believed in this
relationship before. Annette spent a lot of
time with my daughter, caring for her as if
she were her own.

He told me about his past and the change
he had had when he met his new partner.
He married, a career man, who could not
leave his wife. Annette was happy like
that. For those few times they saw each
other she was satisfied, land it was enough
to be loved and desired. Just like every
woman should feel.

I must admit that this new friendship has
opened up different scenarios for me. It
gave me an impulse to reflect on what I
was feeling and experiencing. She was
very sincere and helped me understand
who I was and what I wanted to be.

Meanwhile, Cecìle was increasingly attached to her. They spent a lot of time together. The relationship with Jean deteriorated more and more, as if he had never forgiven me for not telling him right away that I was pregnant.

After all, I've always been a woman who was bothered that a man could treat her like that. And since I was already suffering from this weight gain that I thought was excessive, his words irritated and blocked me.
One evening I had to tell him that things were not going well between us.
"Jean, I have to talk to you"
"Come me, I listen to you" not looking at my face and continuing to eat an ice cream as if to say speak that I do not listen to you.
This also inhibited me.
"I think our relationship doesn't work anymore. I am no longer willing to suffer.

I no longer like your way of doing things, of telling me things. And of how you approach your daughter, you should devote more time to her. More love. Excuse me but that's what I see."

"Coraline, I feel unsuitable to raise a daughter, to take care of this little girl, so it is better that you take care of it, I will give all the financial support possible, because it bears my surname. Sorry I'm going to bed now."

An embarrassment went through my whole body. I couldn't argue.

I thought well not to say anything, I had already understood everything.

"Ah I forgot" also added "Twill you let your new friend help out?"

Here is the final blow. Now also jealousy. I don't know what was going through his mind, I just know that I find myself here rebuilding and my life, with only one joy at my side, Cecìle that will give me the right charge to move forward.

I talked about it with Annette who promptly gave me her help. If had not had her, I would have sunk into a very deep abyss.

I was looking for the strength to react, I lived in the hope of finding love, the true one.

It was certainly not Jean, I am married, I also had a daughter, I do not have to reproach myself for anything, but believing that this farce could continue was not from me.
"You must understand that in life not always the people you meet travel on the same road as you, we women are strong, we can accept, we put the arrow and turn without looking back.

Look at me, two children, a husband who
ran away with a little girl and I here
fighting to rein in my heart that wants to
burst" We hugged very hard.

That hug was worth for me as the
beginning of a new story that would make
my life different. Or at least those were the
intentions. I would have made it.
"Tonight, evening you are at dinner with
us, he will come, and I will introduce him
to you. You will see, you will like it"
I was intrigued and couldn't wait for the
next day to arrive.
"Thanks Annette."

Friendship between women is different from that between men.
We talk about different things.
We dig, we dig...
even if we haven't seen each other for years everything is there where we left it.
Symbiotic hormonal exchanges take place between us.
Where would I be now if I hadn't had my friends."

It's evening, I prepare Cecile and go out to go to Annette. After what is happening between me and Jean, I live lightly, I take what comes. Especially a beautiful friendship like this, happened by chance.

Evidently it was destiny for another woman to approach me and help me clear my mind. And I am so curious to know that the man who, admiring her, timidly reopened his heart. His marriage was not dictated by love, but simply a union.

I saw myself in her story, that's why the curiosity to follow her closely, more intensely.
We women understand each other on the fly, we are different from men, we manage to make hidden feelings flourish that were lost in time. We have that ability to react that sometimes even we don't know where it comes from.

I ring the bell, in spite of a few seconds, a man in his 50s opens to me, very sober, grizzled, of medium stature.

He is a distinguished man, with an evident Italian accent "Hello Coraline, come on, enter, pleasure Maximilian"
"The pleasure is all mine Maximilian, thanks for the invitation I was curious to know her"
"Let's talk about you, we are friends. Annette's friends are also my friends."
I understood Italian well, and I also spoke it. In the family we had Italian relatives and friends on Mom's side. I have always promised myself to visit them, sooner or later I will, but for now I had not had the chance. He makes me sit on the couch, I sit Cecile and immediately asks me if I like something to drink.

Annette is in the bathroom for a shower, and I do not feel any embarrassment to talk to him, indeed, I already like him as a person.

"Annette told me a lot about you and the afternoons you spend at your house."
"Unfortunately, time for us is never enough. The work involves me a lot, I would like to dedicate myself more to her. Do you agree with me that she is an exceptional woman?"

"Yes, Maximilian, I think you are a woman who deserves all the great love you can give. She has not been very lucky in life, the great dignity with which she has carried on the shoulder and the weight of duty to her children, makes her an example to follow"

In those minutes before Annette came out of the bathroom a confidential atmosphere had already been created, and we continued to talk until late at night.

He told me about his current marital situation, and that he could not leave his wife for purely practical reasons, which he could not explain to me, but which had very little to do with love. There were probably some health problems for which he was unable to make his decision.

He is a person who speaks very well, interspersing French Italian, making himself understood very well, I was fascinated. Remained to listen to him with her mouth open, emanated such serenity, in short, a particularly interesting man.

"Now Coraline, I see that you have already made friends? Massimiliano is very empathetic even if he embodies a deep shyness, sometimes he appears shy and reserved with those who do not put him at ease, but it seems that you have made an impression"

And there a little embarrassment has
subsided. What would I have imprinted
on that man? Perhaps. Meanwhile, it was
understood that I was nice to him. I
hadn't had such a peaceful evening for a
long time.

 The daughter slept at a friend's house that
evening, if a form of protection by
Annette, who wanted to pamper herself
Cecìle.
By now I considered her a sister, gave me
tranquility and trust in addition
Maximilian made everything harmonious
with his savoir faire.

We ate, I little for the fixation I had with
the diet, and we also allowed ourselves a
few glasses of good white wine.

We felt like family, Cecile appreciated, but
she already had an adoration for Annette.
Maximilian told me about everything,
looking me straight in the eyes, with that
look that made my head spin.

I didn't tire of staring at him, I smiled, he took me to death, even though I had just met him, he gave me that sense of security that a woman often looks for in her man.

I absolutely did not feel the absence of Jean, who as always had to work. He probably wouldn't have come anyway, and I wouldn't have liked him to be there either, given how things went between us.

Are ally interesting evening, Maximilian was, I began to understand how Annette had fallen in love.
There was immediately a strong understanding between us, I understood that somehow, he too would have aroused changes in me.

The night took over, we said goodbye with speed, and I took Cecile to sleep, it was very late.
Jean was sleeping, we cautiously climbed the stairs trying to make as little noise as possible. I didn't want him to wake up, I wouldn't have endured any more jokes.

Annette opened more and more, told me
about their fairytale encounters, and the
more time passed, the more I wanted to
see him again.

I had that sort of embarrassment for the
desire I felt towards my best friend's lover,
and at the same time if I had him in front
of me, alone, I don't know how I would
have behaved.

I was attracted to him; he represented the
object of desire.

Probably the post-pregnancy, Jean, taking
care of Cecile and my mother, had made
me that effect of canceling myself. Without
realizing it, that sense of frustration
reappeared again, which I always had
within me, that fixation of not being
desired.

Which then connects to the fear of
regaining the lost pounds.

I had gone out early, on a Sunday, it was early April, nature was waking up. As I often did, I took the road to the woods. Morning is my favorite time.

The sun that rises, the colors that fade from blue to purple to leave room for pink, red, and then he arrives, that fiery orange ball, which in a few moments gives life. The first rays penetrate through the trees, forming long bright strips, like lighthouses in a natural stage.

This is my peace.

I lay among the leaves, looking at the sky that is colored blue, among the thick foliage of beech trees.

At one point, I heard a roar of leaves, no one frequented those places at that time, I raised my head and, in the distance, I saw a figure coming towards me.

"Coraline" called in a calm tone.

I believe that in a few moments my
expression has passed from amazement,
pleasure, shame. "Maximilian, what are
you doing here?"
"I didn't know I was back or"

Suddenly that confidence had reappeared,
as if our conversation had picked up
where we had stayed that night.

We had a coffee at the bar down to the
lake, telling each other about our
miserable lives.
There was nothing but a trivial exchange
of telephone numbers that for a long time
neither of them considered important.
If I had to describe the feeling of that day,
well, a book wouldn't be enough.

Inside me, all the certainties were gone,
we had been saying goodbye for half an
hour and I already wanted to call him.

I didn't do it of course, I wouldn't have betrayed Annette or even Jean, they were months, the next few, difficult for me. From one day to the next I became aware that something great was happening to me.

"First you have to empty the bottle, then the soul"

"Hello Coraline, I'm the mother, I need to talk to you, see you in an hour from you?"
"Of course, mom, I'm waiting for you, I'm at home"
When my mother tells me that she wants to talk to me, I have to think of something quite serious, however, something that we should have seriously addressed.

She arrives with a serious attitude, I make her sit down, I offer her a coffee. She loves coffee, especially when we have to talk. Will he have called Dad? Did he know where he was? That was the reason I had imagined, and I was also happy if it was.

"I decided, Coraline. I move to Paris. I plan to do it as early as next week. Remember that house I had near Montmartre. I'll go there. I need it. Here, apart from you, I have no one.

I would be happier staying in Paris, where
I was born and spent so many years of my
life"
"Mom feel free to decide what is right for
you. Don't think about me. I will be able
to cope as I have always done. Also,
because I will have to make decisions
shortly, and I have to do it thinking about
it"

She knew perfectly well that things were
not going well with Jean. I told something,
many things he sensed.

But I have to admit that I wasn't thrilled
that she would go away and leave me
alone. At this moment I would still need
her, even though Annette gave me some
security and closeness.

It was a period, this, that I did not feel
calm. I thought of Cecile so small, but I
tried to react, and I did not dwell on what
awaited me shortly thereafter.
I armed myself with so much courage and
I thought, for a long time.

I imagined an alternative life. Staying at home, on the couch, thinking, I projected myself into a life that was not real but desired. In another place than this one where I live, with another person by my side, with other expectations.

Living an alternative life is good for the heart and soul. It's a situation that makes you much stronger. I wanted to be stronger and think about what I wanted and wanted.

A period began in me in which I absolutely had to make important decisions, made judiciously, because with me there was a little girl and I had to think about her too.
Does taking care of oneself mean being selfish? I think not. I took this step by marrying a man I didn't love but respected, and who turned out to be the opposite of what I wanted.

I gave birth to Cecìle all by myself, raised without the slightest affection from her father. I live with a desire for perennial love. Is it selfishness to afford some life at my age? I don't think anyone can tell me that I can't make dreams come true, because it's about dreams.

I live an inadequacy for the weight that continues to rise, which makes me insecure.

What should I do but give myself a chance, change, modify everything that is currently inside me and also outside.

"Mom do not leave me indifferent, but I must tell you that I cannot hinder you. I can't tell you not to go. I'm worried, a lot. But I have to overcome this too. I have to give myself a limit, I have to think a little about myself"

"Mall of mine you have to forgive me, but like you I also need to take ransoms. I was a mom not up to the situation.

But with you I think I have to be honest to the end. I will not abandon you, moving to Paris is a reason to start living again. I can't see you unhappy with this man, and I'll be close to you for anything. But you must let me go. In the meantime, let's think about the right things to do"

I was already doing it; indeed, I had already done it. At least with thought. I will leave Jean. I will leave that house. I will talk to Annette if she can accommodate me for a while.

I do not know if he will have the chance or the availability. But I have to try.

And after having met her, together with Maximilian, a strong desire was born within me to live them rather than my family, which I would not call such. There is Cecìle. I don't want to be selfish with her. She is my daughter.

Inside me grows the anxiety to rebuild a life, to chase that love that I have been looking for a long time. I made mistakes, and I will start from them. I greeted my mother reassuring her that we will be close in this decision, and she was very happy.

I must say that the cure for his addiction is going well. Thanks to my support. In this I feel proud of myself this sense of help has always been innate in me.

For dinner, when Jean arrived, I put Cecile to bed and sat by her side to talk to him.

"I beg you Coraline another difficult day, I am very tired, I would also like to go to sleep early"

"No, Jean, now you listen to me and very well. I'm tired of all this. For me it's over. I leave you, immediately. In these days I collect all my things and move elsewhere"

"Where are you going? Do you go to your mother? With all the problems she has figured if she welcomes you" This man is a jerk.

He understood nothing about me, about my sense of independence, of autonomy. Especially of freedom. He didn't even understand that I don't love him anymore, or that maybe I never loved him.

His goal is to materialize anything.
He doesn't ask me about Cecile, nor how I feel, how she lives this condition.

He is only interested in organizing things. I'm not with such a man. And I'm leaving.

*"In dreams and love nothing is
impossible"*

I had a strange dream. Pleasant and intriguing at the same time, I liked it so much. It was nothing more than a prelude to a desire, who knows if achievable.

Since I met Maximilian to Annette, I happened to dream of him in a recurring way.

Although much older than me, he was a person who aroused deep interest and admiration in me.

He had presented himself very politely, his way of doing things excited me, I saw him as a person to be taught by, almost a teacher of life. Yet, I had just met him.

I felt like a little girl to whom they had given a box of chocolates.

I dreamed of making love to him. There were no other details. It was an unbridled desire on my part to do it, and we did it all the time.

It was not only dreaming of it that made this irrepressible desire grow in me.

We spoke on the phone, he called me one morning, he was in Italy, of course I didn't tell him anything, I was ashamed. He spoke to me softly, with such kindness, I felt him really close, he cared about me, as no one had done so far.

There was in me this great desire to experiment, to live it. I don't know what took me. Such a desire to escape from the usual routine, from this marriage that was now coming to an end.

I thought of Annette, of her blindly trusting me, I felt guilty, just thinking. I was totally taken.

I kept dreaming of it, and every time it was more and more beautiful. More and more intense. We made love with so much passion and feeling, even though it was just a dream, it seemed so real.

I felt small in front of him. It was not for the years of difference, it was precisely because of his sense of experience, which revealed a sweet soul and at the same time cruel and tried by events.

I didn't feel up to it. I didn't like my body. And so, I thought he wouldn't like it either. This conditioned me very much, and what was happening between me, and my husband lasted me more and more towards him.

I thought about it all the time and not being able to own it made me nervous, dissatisfied. It wasn't falling in love with mine.

It was the desire to own it. In dreams it was like this, I felt very strong and sensual, as I had never been in my life, and I received from him what I wanted, fire and passion. I don't think I ever made love like in those dreams.

This was also a spring that made me make the drastic decision to leave Jean. After a week, which we had talked about, I was already living at Annette's house.
With Jean we had thought of taking care of the good of the child, and to live our lives separately, in the most serene way possible. Only now, my problems had increased.

I had to find a job, support Cecile, and contribute with Annette to the daily needs of living together.

It would not have been a long time, because in my mind the idea of leaving, changing my life, in another city, where I could be reborn without prejudice, flashed in my mind.

A thousand thoughts were running through my head. How would I have done on those occasions when Maximilian showed up at home?

I would have experienced a great embarrassment, but above all, would I have been disloyal to Annette?

What if in my crazy head I had approached Maximilian as I did in a dream?
But inside me I had already decided.

I had to find my dimension, to live these experiences never lived before. Make my life less heavy.

"Annette I just wanted to tell you that I will stay for a while, I do not want to condition your life and the relationship with Maximilian"

"Coraline, I've already spoken to him. There are no problems, we will face this coexistence together. I realized that there is a good understanding between you.

Have you felt more since that time I introduced it to you? Maybe you had a coffee together, he told me"

"No, Annette we haven't heard from since that time. He is your man and I do not allow myself to invade your sphere"

I lied. I don't know what got me at the time, I didn't even think I was capable of it.

I had a fear of ruining everything by telling her about dreams and that morning's phone call from Italy. I even though he knew and put me to the test.

I took a risk, maybe, he tells her everything, and he will have told her this too.

But I didn't regret that lie for good. We kept talking about how we could organize and support each other.

From that moment on, a chapter of my life
was closing. Another one opened and
perhaps to follow many other small
chapters that I needed to write.
The moment of revolt had begun, with
myself, and with everything around me.

My life would reset at that moment, even
though I would never throw away the
memories.
More than anything for me it did not mean
canceling but putting a point and starting
again.

And I was coming to life again, I wanted
to love, dream, return to the center of me,
dedicate time, and enjoy the little things.

"What you can't turn into something wonderful, you have to let it go"

I was upset that night. I didn't feel calm. The idea of taking my things, of leaving the place where I had spent my life until now, left a little bitter in my mouth.

I commissioned a friend of Mom's to take things and take them to her in Paris.

Cecile and I will have taken a train. <<Ready Jean? Hello, I wanted to warn you that we are going. I will let you know my mother's address and contacts if you want to see Cecile. For me there is no impediment. I think that's right. I'm sorry for what happened but I must go. >>

On the other side of the phone a disarming silence. I had the impression that he was crying.
"Jean what's there? You don't tell me anything. What's going on with you?"

He couldn't speak, he hung up. I felt bad about the pain I was causing him. But I couldn't look back, I had to continue my way.

I would have sent him all the necessary contacts to see Cecile. I think he's doing the right thing. My decision was made. I was sorry, but I had to focus on the goal I had set for myself: to start living again.

I close the door of that house, already knowing that I would not reopen it, probably forever.

I was planning to leave the keys to the neighbor, but I didn't want to give rise to gossip.
I greet Alfred who leaves with his van for Paris, he had just accompanied me to the station, a small trolley, Cecile and we leave. I sit at the carriage in front, it had to be the 2.

I am told to me by an elderly lady who is watching me.

___

"What a beautiful girl you are, you are going where your heart takes you, or am I wrong?"

"So, you're ma'am? I don't understand. I don't know if we ever met, or at least I don't think so"

"No, we never met, my name is Adrien. I notice on your face a desire for escape, I feel it. I have a good intuition. I think I guessed it. That's not true?"

"My name is Coraline, has really seen well"

That was one of the many situations in which I met people, observed them, and thought I had always known them and that they knew everything about me.

This gave me the courage to start again, the good feelings that people had of me supported me.
I arrive in Paris in the evening, my mother is waiting for me.
At Gare de Lyon station.

I didn't know that area, or I don't remember it. We walked along Boulevard Diderot until we reached Nation. He lived there, in a narrow street called Passage du Trone.

She came by car with a neighbor. We arrive, I leave my things and take a nice shower. As if to take away the heaviness of this day.

Let's talk a bit, she also feels bad about Jean's reaction. She was a very sensitive woman, despite the fact that she showed dryness, but deep down she was.
Cecile is as if she were at home, she easily adapts to transfers.

I had therefore decided to leave Cecile to my mother. And she was very happy with this, there was a good relationship of complicity between them, it pleased her, and she could finally in her life reciprocate my help.

—

I did not feel guilty, nor did I have the scruple of having abandoned her to who knows who.
I told her that I would give Jean all the contacts and she agreed to welcome him whenever she wanted.

It was his father. I didn't want to become like other wives who prevent their husbands from seeing their children.

I didn't get to that. Jean was basically a good guy, he had just disappointed me a little, but he wasn't bad, he had never been. He was just not the man for me, and this was understood.

I stay with her for about ten days, just enough time to arrange my things, organize Cecile and decide what to do, where to go, what life to go.

I had also warned Annette before leaving. I had gone to say goodbye to her, for her it had been a bit of a difficult day, she did not want me to abandon her.

She welcomed me almost crying, she suffered, the detachment for her was a torture, after the one with her husband. He seemed to be fine with Maximilian anyway, or at least that was what I thought. He had been missing for some time. He was more often in Italy, and they could not see each other frequently.

This impossibility of leaving his wife continued. I understand Annette's difficulty in living a normal love life, these ups and downs made her less and less stable.

If you add that I was also leaving, an absurd fear of being alone was unleashed in her.

I had to say goodbye. She understood that I needed a new life, to find myself, and above all to make sense of my things. The weight had become for me a boulder, from which to free myself soon.

I didn't know exactly where to go. There were several options.

I had also thought about approaching
Lorenne. She was a childhood friend of
mine; we had grown up as sisters.
He lived in Juvignac.

We spent a lot of time together. We have
always confided everything to each other.
We attended the same class, and very
often we studied together, at his home. He
had a brother who was a couple of years
older. Her mother had died when she was
very young, her life had been spent with
her father who had never remarried.

She had met a man older than her,
separated, who had convinced her to
move to Italy, to Florence.

They met at a time when, for work, he had
moved to Montpellier for a couple of
years. Then finished the work he returned
to Italy bringing Lorenne with him.

I never liked that man. She was very
sweet, a woman with a good soul. He may
not have treated her as she deserved.

This disturbed me, creating in me a sense
of protection and defense towards her that
had always been so fragile.
I remember that day he decided to go to
Italy, the tears we made, one of the sad
days fixed in my memory.

"Coraline always remember me, even
when I am in Italy. Take care of yourself
and be surrounded by people who want
your good. I chose so, not being able to do
otherwise. I no longer feel comfortable
here, my father I see him very tired and
sick there will be my brother at his side, he
himself told me to go and make me a more
serene life. Growing up without the
support of a mom was not easy, now I
need someone to take care of me. Coraline,
chase your dreams, chase what you want
and that makes you feel good"

I promised her that I would visit her one
day.

In the meantime, we wrote to each other, phone calls, video calls. He lived in a small villa just outside Florence. A beautiful place, with views of the hills that were very reminiscent of our origins.
She was almost always alone, the partner worked a lot, but she was somehow happy. She had her own world, her apparent loneliness made her even stronger. He didn't need anything else. This is what you could guess from our endless chats.

A year ago, she had a bone disease, I never understood exactly what it was, but she was being treated to alleviate it.

He would have made further investigations.
That's why he wanted to see me as soon as possible. That wasn't the place I wanted to live, but I would go and visit her. I missed him to death.
Now I had to decide, another opportunity was to talk to Maximilian.

I didn't know where he worked, but somehow, I knew he could help me. I wanted to call him. I would have done it, also to hear him and tell him that I was moving to Italy, after all that dream was still in my head, along with the desire to have it.
I just had to find out where he was in Italy.

What interested me most now, however, was to do something for my weight.

I kept getting fat and I didn't see myself as beautiful, I didn't see myself as what I wanted to be. I couldn't do things I wanted, I had to take the situation by the hand.

I had talked about it with my mother, but she, like many others, had easily suggested that I do a diet and physical activity. The usual advice of those who do not understand the discomfort of being overweight, or worse obese.

I informed myself, I read, I documented
myself. I wanted to do something at all
costs. I pushed myself to do it in Italy,
even if in France I would have found
suitable centers. I felt the need to do it
away from everyone and everything.
I had the courage to call Maximilian.
"Hello, how are you? I hope not to bother
you"

"No Coraline does not bother me at all,
indeed I really wanted to hear you. I
thought I'd come to Annette tomorrow,
and if you want, we can see each other"

"No Maximilian, I am in Paris, at my
mother's. I decided to leave Juvignac, I
took Cecile and I came here. I leave my
daughter to my mother, and I plan to
move to Italy, I don't know where yet, but
I'm convinced to do it"

"I'm sorry that things went like this,
Coraline. I am in France now, but I will be
in Italy in about ten days, we have a
construction site to check in Chioggia. Let
me know where you go that if I can help
you in some way. However, I reach you, I
want to hug you."
These words had given me an incredible
charge, I am like that, if
I start a dream I would never want to
wake up.

This interest had given me security. I
would find myself a job, explore the area
and then write down my future.
Meanwhile, there was him who had
shown himself available.

He might have said it to Annette, since he
was going to visit her, but I didn't care.

I wasn't sure if their relationship was
going well. But this, to tell the truth, was
not important to me now, and not to
Annette, but because I should have started
thinking about myself, about my things. I
had priorities.

After two days, I decide to take the train, two small suitcases in my wake, and here I am on my way to Chioggia. Yes, I had decided to go there. I had inquired about the city, I was not sure that I would like it, but I had to start moving in the meantime.

I had also spotted a nearby center that would cure my obesity.
I said goodbye to my mom, hugged Cecile tightly, reassuring her that I would be out for a while and that I would take her back as soon as possible.

She was sad, but she realized that I was not able to devote myself to her at that moment. I felt my heartbeat like never before.

Leaving Cecìle, starting a new life, with new expectations, electrifies me.
I lived these moments with great intensity, because finally my life, my future, was in my hands.

I took the train at 8pm from Bercy. I traveled all night to arrive at lunchtime.

I had found a small hotel for a week just to get to know the area, and then found myself a cheaper accommodation in an apartment.

My new adventure begins here.

***"You can always leave and sometimes it
is necessary"***

It's a June afternoon, it's very hot. Sitting
by the sea, next to the port, I enjoy the last
moments of sunshine.

I arrived here a few days ago, I have to
start settling in, getting to know, making
my days more intense.
Because that's exactly what I need.

Memories go through my mind, I would
like to keep them in a trunk, arrange them
and take them if necessary.

Today I would like to be like this, without
thinking about anything. Stay here in front
of the sun waiting for the sunset.

I order a coffee, the usual, long, bitter, that
will keep me company, that will make me
scrutinize the sea and gallop with fantasy.

In a bar of yesteryear, with some tables in
the little space in front, I observe a leaf
fallen on the uneven floor, and I think that
something beautiful will happen,
something that will give me the push to
start again, to make my life more
beautiful, more harmonious.

A lady arrives and sits at the table next to
mine. She is a distinguished lady, blonde,
very beautiful. Definitely more beautiful
than me, as I see myself right now.
He lights a cigarette and smokes with
class. Order a rum.

I observe it carefully, it makes me curious,
but I try not to be seen. I keep watching
trying to pretend nothing.

There is too much curiosity towards that
woman, I have the feeling that I have
already known her. As if in another life it
had belonged to me.
She turns around and addresses me
"Hello". I respond to the greeting with a
smile.

He invites me to sit at his table, as does a
man when he invites a woman to dine
with him in a restaurant. It has a
noticeable impact on me, those big, green,
transparent eyes, I felt embarrassed in
front of that look.

As if somehow, I was attracted to it.
I gladly accept, leaving my coffee in half, I
order another I think to myself, indeed no,
I think again, I prefer to order a rum and
keep her company.

I introduce myself: I'm Coraline, and I'm
new here, I don't know anyone, I'm glad
he invited me to his table.

She replies: "I'm Rebecca. And give me
some you. I seem to have already seen
you. It intrigued me how you looked at
me."
And I understood that she had noticed.
That moment was the beginning of our
acquaintance.

Rebecca is a married lady, with a son, of
age.

She is a restless woman, you can see it
from afar, without even needing to talk to
us.

Classy, very well cared for, she is more or
less my age, it is pleasant to talk to her, a
colorful soul even if with dark traits.

Maybe I had found the person who would
take me on the road I wanted. Yet, I had
just met her, but I already felt connected to
her.

He emanated a sense of harmonious
security, I cannot explain, his beauty
enriched his determined character, and his
words came directly from a wounded but
healthy heart, a balance chased for years,
it was understood.

I had discovered that some people gave
me a particular energy and I noticed in me
aspects that were closed, I do not know
where, for a long time.

I told her about my past, about my life in France, and about this desire to go away to find myself, to find that love that was holed up inside me and that did not want to go out to be recognized.

When we talked about loves I saw that she was crying, some tears were running down her face. It made me very tender. But above all I wondered why I didn't cry.

At that moment she told herself. I was absorbed in his words, which were for me a great reflection of how a love can make you suffer and rejoice at the same time.

It was his story, but I made it my own, as if I myself had to retrace his footsteps. The relationship with her husband was very conflictual, extinguished by now, without transport.

For a woman this lack is very strong and significant. Feeling desired, loved, pampered, this is what makes her feel good, which stimulates her to open up and express her passion and feelings to the maximum.

Here I immersed myself in his story, as if he were talking about my life. But I was attracted to the sequel.

From how he would react to this lack of love. Because you could see that she was a woman who could love immeasurably, she believed it.

As every woman should do believe in love. And she always believed in it.

"Coraline, I have always thought that in a woman's life there should be a man able to support her, to love her and above all to make her feel like a woman, I grew up with these expectations."

"But now I believe that these things that you expect from a man you must look for yourself, you have to make sure that they come or go and get them. They must be a conquest, a trophy. Because man loves as long as he can, as long as he is satisfied, until it becomes obvious."

Rebecca spoke a lot, and I was fascinated by her craving for love, which was a bit like mine.

It was not like having a man to us, but a search for care, attention, small gestures that made her feel unique.

Here, the respect that Rebecca carried for her body was the same that she wanted to receive from a man, and this was not happening, she felt alone, her husband did not understand these needs.

Men are basically made like this, he said.
And it is you woman who must attract
them, who must make them excited. Their
share of hunters stops when they know a
woman and make her their own. But then?
Who knows what the then has in store for
us.

The thing that made her most angry was
precisely this possession that a man
believes he has once he has seduced you.

She kept telling about her family, about
this flat, cold relationship that was making
her age ahead of time.
And I listened to him carefully, I wanted
to grasp all the decisive aspects that would
make me know who he really was.

But the best thing was that he spoke to me
as if he were confiding in his sister, in
reality he had a natural one who lived
abroad but had not seen it for years.

These words of hers for me were sap, I
had found in her an ally. A teacher of life.
There was understanding already after a
few minutes that we were talking.

Meanwhile our rum was almost finished.
But we didn't get up, we decided to keep
talking to each other. A gap had opened,
and an immense desire to tell us.

She felt a great affinity with me. We were
just talking about her. I had told her little,
very little except to introduce myself. But
my time would come soon.

"Coralinc, a beautiful name, beautiful as
the sun, intriguing, mysterious."
"It's true Rebecca, it's like that, evidently it
suits me"
"I would like to tell you something. I trust
you"
"I thank you; can you tell me everything,
I'm here for you"

Our conversation now shifted to rather intriguing private facts, such as to arouse a certain particular interest in listening to her. A woman like this may never have happened to me to know her.

And from that moment on, it was a lot of talk. I saw in her a person who could open my eyes to new realities. She had become my confidant.

Rebecca marries young, her husband is a man engaged in politics, a successful manager. She, a woman of many interests and endless initiatives. After two years of marriage, Alberto was born.

She dedicates herself to him, to the house, in short, to his life as a mother and wife.

She is not satisfied, she needs different, stronger emotions. The relationship with her husband is increasingly fought.

He is always out, for work, for political commitments or other, this generates in Rebecca an increasingly evident dissatisfaction.

He does not live as he would have liked. He couldn't find the love he wanted. She loved her husband, but it didn't make her happy. Even their relations had gradually weakened, almost absent.

She suffered a lot from all this, she was looking for an experience that made her feel loved but above all important. She always had the need to heal herself, to have fun, to feel alive while her family context bordered on boredom.

Here is what he told me, alternating a cigarette and a sip of excellent rum. It had

gone from a very strong one, to a softer and more fragrant one.
And his voice became more and more intense, he was excited while he told himself, in those fabulous green eyes you could see all his experience pass.

I watched it and listened to it with great interest. I drew lessons, we were very close.
"Coraline, women like us need to feel the love inside, the warmth. Superficiality for us is inner death. It is the end of a desire that starts from afar. I decided to feel different emotions, to live myself and to live a different experience, much more enveloping"

What did he mean? In this story he let an emotional part shine through. He stopped, lowered his head almost perhaps out of embarrassment with the things he was about to say.

She felt unfit to have other experiences, to betray what was her primary desire: to love her husband.

This was what I read in his eyes. I saw her strong, but very fragile. It wasn't quite what he wanted. But circumstances had led her to that situation.

He thought it would be a passing cloud, which would unleash lightning as in a strong thunderstorm, and once he passed away, he was afraid of returning to reality, which seemed the right thing, but it was certainly not what he dreamed of.

What was he talking about? Of a love met by chance? That's what he was talking about. And I was there to watch her, to extend a hand to her because I wanted her to feel it.

"I met this man about 15 years ago. We were neighbors. She was a beautiful person, and she was with a friend of mine forever. They were very much in love, I could feel it, we even dated as a couple for a while"

"Rebecca, even then you felt something for him? Did you feel an attraction?"
I immediately preferred to ask this question to see if she was already attracted to it, I wanted her story to be mine.

"No Coraline, absolutely not. I had great respect for his wife's friendship. And then I was in love with my husband. I had a good relationship with him, quite intense."

Things changed later. He told me.
"He, my husband I mean, was very busy in work" had no interest in her, in a beautiful woman with whom he was evidently in love but there was no longer the initial desire.

After all, the reports go even like this.
People are not always destined to age
together.

"It was an early morning, just before 6
a.m. I got a message

*Hello, I would like to see you, I would like to
have a coffee alone with you. Would you like?*

This stealthy invitation excited me. I was
curious, I wanted to understand why that
invitation alone, and not with his wife, my
lifelong friend"

"We saw each other, one afternoon in July,
it was very hot. I waited for him in a bar,
he also took a while. I thought he would
not come again. I would never have called
him. I had a great anxiety in me that grew.
It was like it was my first date with a man.
A special feeling."

"I saw him coming, he was beautiful, radiant. He smiled like someone who had to meet his own woman.
It never passed to me for a moment the thought that I was doing something wrong.
Curiosity and the desire to meet him surpassed everything.
It was a very strange situation, an emotion that took me that I had never felt.

Yet, I had known him for a long time. I was definitely agitated. We took a prosecco both, and talked, talked, talked. He explained to me his relationship with his wife.

He made me understand that he cared about me, that he had been thinking about me for quite a while. And I was happy to be desired. A feeling that I had forgotten by now. Strangely enough, I didn't care what might happen."

"Rebecca, have you never felt wrong?
Even if only to have a drink together and
talk about your things secretly?

After all, she was one of your best friends,
what went on in you, what did you feel at
that moment? Probably I would never
have succeeded, in that situation,
friendship for me has a lot of value.

Don't misunderstand, I'm not saying I
don't have it for you, I'm just saying I
wouldn't see myself."

Probably this was just an interpretation of
what my brain wanted to say, but my
heart thought something else; he dreamed
of diving into an ocean of stolen kisses,
tight hugs, and long nights of passion in
the moonlight.

The day had lost its sense of time and space.

As if we were in a dimension only ours, suspended on our fairy tales. It was the third glass of rum, all the glass between us was falling.

"Coraline, no one knows my story, maybe you can understand what I feel. Our first real date was memorable."

We had to meet in the morning, to arouse less suspicion. It was an unusual thing for me, who was used to telling everything to my best friend.

It was half past eight, we were both in our respective cars, in a remote parking lot in Mestre.
The rain was pouring like never before, I had even ironed my hair. Neither of them had the courage to get off, then I decided and with my high heels and coat I approached his window.

The rain had completely wet me, he
opened the door slightly and told me *what
you do out there, you will take an accident.*

I got into his car, like a chick just out of the
egg, on my face the water still came down
from my hair, he passed his hands on my
cheeks as if to dry me and with absolute
lightness he brought my face to himself
and kissed me.

I can't express what I felt at that moment,
it wasn't just a kiss, it contained a
thousand shades of passion. It didn't take
more than five minutes that we were
making love, there in the car like the kids.

There was an attraction and complicity
that I had never experienced with anyone.
I still remember its scent that stuck on me
for hours after we said goodbye.

It was noon and we still had not spoken to
each other, that is, we had not spoken a
word but only intense, unforgettable
looks, it was an incredible morning that I
will never forget. That was the beginning
of our love story, which continued with
long messages.

"Home is where the heart is"

I settled in Chioggia in a small hotel, for a week, I would have found a solution shortly.
Meanwhile, I missed my things and Cecile, whom I heard three times a day on the phone. But I had in mind what I had to do.
Knowing Rebecca had opened my mind. I wanted to fall in love, to believe that there was something or someone destined for me. I know he was there, and I had to pick him up.
The priority now, however, was to do something for my weight. I could no longer bear this obesity that grew in me, not only aesthetically, I felt awkward, even in relationships with people, I was sad because I wanted immediate results, I did not have time to wait, the time was now.
I found a center that treats eating disorders and obesity. It's right by here. I decided to go there.

That evening, at the appointment, there was a young surgeon, very professional. He made me feel comfortable, we talked about how I felt, and what I expected, then he explained to me how I could overcome this weight that was troubling me.

He proposed bariatric surgery, more precisely the Sleeve Gastrectomy. He synthesized to me that there would be a resection of the stomach. Only a third would be left.

I wasn't very sure, I didn't know these things, but it was probably the right solution.

I talked about it with Rebecca first, then with my mother.

They did not express their opinion, they let me decide, after all, these are things that you have to feel inside, only you can feel that feeling of having touched the bottom.

I decide to take this path, also psychological. And so, without delay I was on the list. Meanwhile, I organized my things, a possible job, I began to fit into this new reality that would give me the right push to start living again. Intervention would have been indispensable in this process of change.

"Mother hello. I decided, I do the Sleeve"
"Coraline if you think it's the right thing do it. I help you in everything, even economically if you need it."
These words cheered me up a bit. My situation was not one that could make you feel comfortable. Evidently my mother knew where to draw. I never knew anything about his income. I can only think that he had access to some family treasure. I was his daughter, and it could only please me.

I called Maximilian again, my thoughts always led to him. He was glad that I had come to Italy, and to Chioggia.

It was no coincidence. He worked there, and I would have had the chance to see him easily.

However, days had passed, and we hadn't met yet. I also had his support for the intervention, and of course he was present if I needed it.

"If you want, Coraline, we can see each other on Sunday. I will reach you if you tell me where you are"
Excited I replied with a trivial thumbs up.

There were two days left before that Sunday, a great anxiety grew in me. See secretly from Annette intrigued me a lot.

I told Rebecca about this as well. She smiled and urged me to do it, after all she understood me very well given her tangled sentimental situation.

———

Do you want to see this meeting? This
man at the time gave me a feeling of well-
being, to see him dreamed of several times
in particular situations increased my
desire to see him.

He was much older than me, but it didn't
bother me. I was only interested in
understanding what I would feel standing
there in front of him.

I wanted to see if my heart feels the same
sensations I felt in dreams.

Losing weight was also a dream.

The intervention was getting closer and
closer, and so was the meeting with
Maximilian.

That Sunday it must have been nine in the
morning, I left my hotel, where I was still
staying, and moved to the port.

I waited for it to arrive right on the edge of
a quay. He did not wait long, after a few
minutes he arrived.

Sporty, with jeans. He almost did not prove the age he was.

"Hello Cecile how are you?"
"Well Maximilian, you are in perfect shape. As you see I succeeded I started a new life. Let's hope things go well."
"Let's go to me. I'll show you where I live when I'm here."

And immediately my heart began to beat fast.

We went to his house. He had a small apartment near the port. There when he came to Italy.
It was very pretty, nicely decorated. A studio apartment on a single scale.

He made me sit on his couch and offered me coffee. He was very kind, more than when we had met at Annette's.

We also talked about her. And in me grew the anxiety that maybe I was doing something shady, impure towards my friend.

______

I looked at his eyes and saw that there was
something that attracted me.
At the crossroads of outgazes we kissed.
It was a spontaneous, natural thing
intensely

I let myself go, without thinking too much
about it, just like in my dreams.
For once I thought of myself.

I liked this situation too much.
He guided me to his bed. It was evident
that the goal was that.

We made love like I had never done
before.
It was just sex, a very strong attraction, I
think he thought so too.

It was what I had experienced in so many
dreams, thinking that they would never
come true.
We did it several times, he was a vigorous
man. It was beautiful, I felt the object of
his desire, as he was for me.

After it happened, I wanted it even more.

He confessed to me that he had wanted him since we met. He also asked me if I liked it.

I told him yes, I would have told him anyway. I felt a little guilty about Annette, but I was reflecting on the fact that we would see each other again, just like in dreams.

"Don't choose what's easy, choose what's worth it"

It was worth it. I felt like the protagonist of a movie in a scene, after an intense love relationship. That's what I felt.

I found myself a little more than a year after my move to Italy, in Chioggia, with a job in an IT company, as a consultant in administration. About 35 kg lost because of bariatric surgery.

Practically another person, full of spirit, with a different soul.
I heard Cecile almost every week, on the phone, I promised her that I would go to Paris to visit her.

Meanwhile, she grew up with my mother, who devoted all the necessary care to her.

I had become a different woman. What I
wanted was to start an evolutionary path.

Starting with my health. Because it all
starts when you become aware that you
have to do something to solve the problem
at the root.
I was breaking that shell.
I had found a home in the suburbs. A
small two-bedroom apartment,
comfortable, to my measure. Tastefully
decorated and improved by me.

These were hard days, the first few months
after the operation. I had to take a winding
road made of limitations, of restrictions
because of an obligatory medical
indication.

I wanted and had to feel good, there was no
other way.
And the results were not long in coming.
My body was different, it was a body that
I began to recognize.

And my way of thinking had definitely
changed.

———

Maximilian was also important for my new life in Italy, we saw each other other later, he wanted me even before I lost weight, let alone then.

Time passed and the desire did not go out, it must have been a whim, but it was becoming something more, at least on my part. Later I realized that he was not the love I was looking for, or that I wasn't really looking for love.

At some point, I stopped calling him, and so did he. After all, there was no hope for us, he already had a wife and a lover, and maybe even someone else.

This period marked a change in me, and the realization that I could get what I wanted, and let it go when I no longer wanted it.

Things weren't going well with Annette. She needed to see him more often. Which did not happen. He did not want to leave his wife, sick, in need of care.

I never told Annette that we saw each other, I didn't feel like telling her the truth, even though I loved her very much, even for what she had done for me and Cecìle.

Our phone calls were beginning to be less frequent. I had to focus on my new life, be careful about what I had to face, keep tight the work I had managed to get that made me live with dignity.

The thought was however towards the search for a new dimension, the one that would allow me to find a love, as I wanted it. Would I have succeeded?

———

With Rebecca, we have seen each other many times. She continued her acquaintance with the man who did not leave her alone. There, too, there continued to be an unclear situation, and she was very worried about it.

She lived these days overcome by the remorse of betraying her husband and at the same time entertaining herself with a person with whom she could not understand if it was a relationship of love or infatuation with the forbidden.

To tone my body and lighten my mind I decided to enroll in a course of Tai Chi Chuang, a Chinese version of yoga, with slow movements.

The master, Chinese from Whangtzu, was a little man in his fifties, very good and experienced. That would also have been an opportunity to meet new people.

After the surgery I was always quite alone with myself, with my rebirth. Apart from those occasions of meeting with Massimiliano and Rebecca, there was no other attendance on my part. This was the time to meet people, and approach new bonds.

I immediately notice a girl; she must have been the same age as me. He was always in front of me, looking at me and smiling.

I responded to his smiles. We also laughed with taste at some wrong movement that distracted us from what was the teaching of the master.

It was a beautiful discipline; it drives
away thoughts.
At the shower, he approaches me.
"Pleasure my name is Angela, you?"
"Coraline"
"You aren't Italian? I feel a French
inflection"
"You are, in fact I French, moved just over
a year ago here in Italy"
We went out, sat on a wall, and talked a
lot, she told me about her.

She was born in Switzerland, her
emigrants were of Italian origin, as many
in those years had gone in search of
fortune. He had a carefree childhood, he
told me about the long days spent running
in the green mountains, and the hours
spent in the gym to become an étoile test
tube.

She spoke of Switzerland with regret that
she had not stayed there. She was a
woman who knew how to involve with
her stories, she had an incredible mastery
of language, with somewhat German
inflections, she knew how to take breaks
and changes in intensity to make the story
exciting.

Then I understood why. She was a theater
actress, and this profession had brought
her back to Italy victim of some financial
misadventure, she was like me, looking
for her own spirit to find within herself
that strength to react and start living
again.

She was passionate about shamanism, she

introduced me to many people in the area, with whom she met for activities like the one we were doing together.
A deep friendship was born, we shared a lot in that period.

She was enrolled in one of those platforms where comrades are sought, she insisted with me that I do it too. But it wasn't so important to me, if I happened to date someone well, otherwise I would take care of myself.

I had become my priority now. Always for his innate force of persuasion he convinced me, one evening, to go to a meeting of four that he had procured at that site.

I satisfied her this time; we went out with the two most boring men on earth. At ten o'clock I faked an illness and we left them to go dancing.
"Coraline where are we going? Come on you decide, I've already done enough damage tonight"

I wasn't good at dancing, I felt like a seal, even though my body had changed I always felt clumsy.

But she wanted to have fun, she needed to go a little over the top. << I have an idea, why don't we go to that place on the island of Pellestrina, the one Rebecca told me about, you have understood which one, the one frequented by homosexuals>>
"If you care we go, but you know how I think, as boring as boring, I always prefer men."

It was fog in the lagoon, The last motorboat for Pellestrina left at twenty-three, we did the races, but we made it.

"Coraline is so much that you insist on coming to this place, is it not that by chance the intervention made you change sides?"

"Angela, I don't know, everything has
changed inside me, my dreams, my
desires, my way of interacting with
people, I met a girl on the net.
I am very attracted to her, her name is
Cloe, she told me a little about her life, she
is fascinating, she has a sweetness mixed
with shyness seasoned with a pinch of
irony, I love her. He told me he was
homosexual."

Well, yes, although far away I had tried
with her. It was naturally spontaneous,
but she does not live with the lightness
with which I am living, and she
immediately crushed me, telling me that
mine was just a whim. I told her that
instead I had the doubt that I could also be
like her.

So, he advised me to start going to some
homosexual club to see my reaction live
and actually understand who I have
become.

"From moving we enter Angela, now that we are here" she was reluctant, all those beautiful girls younger than us who danced. I, on the other hand, was thrilled.

A bit 'all the new things gave me euphoria. This status of physical well-being pushed me to dare, especially with my body.

I found myself, after a couple of cocktails, wriggling in a box, and laughing like a fool. There was a skinny blonde woman with beautiful blue eyes.

It was approaching, oh my God, my legs were shaking, a new experience, my heart was beating like when I was a little girl. "Can I offer you a drink?" he said to Me in a very sweet and calm voice. Obviously, I could not refuse, I left the scene and ran to the counter reaching it. "Pleasure my name is Coraline"
"You are beautiful Coraline"

 She didn't even leave me time to ask her what her name was that an American had already ordered me. I blush at his statement; I was used to men who before giving you a compliment must take measures. "Like it here? There are not many equipped beaches on the island, but for me who love nature and lying under the sun completely naked by the sea is a spectacle.

I have been living here for a couple of years, I have found my paradise. By the way, so much pleasure, my name is Delia" We had gone out, we looked at the sea, it was a mild evening, a bit humid, as always in these areas.

Without realizing it, he approached me and began to kiss me, immediately I pulled back but slowly I began to savor that transgression.

Everything was limited to that intense and pleasant kiss. It was a long night, there was no means to go back, Delia offered us her sofa and we spent the night there.

"The most difficult task in life is to change oneself"

"Mom, I'm at 2 pm at Paris Bercy>>
"What a nice surprise, Coraline. I'm glad
to see you. I'll be there with Cecile"
Having met my daughter and mother after
a long time, and especially after my
journey, was an infinite joy for me.

Cecile ran to hug me, happy to see me. She
had grown up, a lot, she had really
become a beautiful girl, although for me
she will always be a child, my little girl!

"Coraline you are an enchantment; you
are very well. I'm proud of you. Will you
stay a few days? I prepare the room for
you; you will want to sleep with the little
one I guess"

"Of course, Mom, I'll want to sleep with her. I want to enjoy it for a few days, I will be forced to leave in three days. I'm working, I can't stay out too long. I have taken advantage of it now. I wanted to see you."

We talked a lot, I asked her about my
father. He confirmed to me that he was
out, he was fine, and he had asked about
me.

He had reassured him by telling him
about my changes, that I had managed to
settle in Italy, that I had made the Sleeve
and that I was quiet and starting to live
again. He was very sorry for what
happened with Jean, who in the meantime
had moved to Rouen, in the north of
France.

He lived with a new partner, separated,
with two children older than him. He
came to visit Cecile almost every week.

My mother always welcomed him with
pleasure and gave him the opportunity to
spend a few hours with her daughter.
In short, an update of lives, I was serene to
know that things were going well for
everyone, but a doubt assailed me: that
famous secret that my mother kept about
my father.

"Mommy you have to tell me something.
I'm ready now, maybe it's time to talk
about it, don't you think?"

"Yes Coraline, I think that time has come.
I've kept it safe for many years, but now
it's really time to tell you everything."
He will tell me about an important thing,
which will upset me, but he could no
longer hide.

My father was not my natural father. He told me that at the time the relationships were not splendid.

She wanted a child, but she did not arrive, with him evidently there was some problem. And then he thought well of procreating with another person, whom he never saw again.

Who doesn't even know who he is, and where he is? Like all women at some point in her life she had a great desire for motherhood. At first, I was speechless, even a tear slipped through me.

But I understood my mother on this occasion too. He did it for his own good. It was not a betrayal, but the need to have a child.

She thought well of telling my father that she was pregnant with him, and he was happy for this, because he was like that, it took little to make him happy.

I forgave my mother for what she did. I hugged her tightly and we cried a lot, not of pain, but of emotion. Cecile was not present; she would have been very bad.

This secret also revealed enriched me. It entered forcefully into my life of renewal that I was pursuing.

It was a sign that I had to live everything that came with intensity, this news meant a lot to me. I also understood those painful moments, when my mother clung to alcohol, and that strong character that covered a sensitivity that showed itself over time.

These are things that I collect, I make my own, my wealth of experiences that lead me to understand what my future will be.

I told her about Rebecca, my work life, Cloe and Maximilian, whom she knew as Annette's partner.
We were hurt. He thought it was a bad experience, and that it wouldn't lead me to anything good.

___

I told her that this relationship would
have no absolute value, but only sex.
I was really hoping for a complete love,
something that would change my life
permanently, but it was not indispensable.

I felt the need, for what I was becoming,
for the woman I wanted to be. But if it
wasn't such, I would have done without it,
I was no longer the kind of woman who
needed a man.

She understood me, as a mother does in
front of her daughter, and she agreed.
Annette had called her a few days earlier.

He had told her that he was no longer good
with Maximilian and that he had not felt
with me for quite a while.

I confirmed that this was the case, that I
had not told her that I had seen each other
with him.

"He also told me, that he had the feeling that the two of you had been together. He had warned him. He had already sniffed it when you were there, how you looked at each other, how you spoke to each other." I realized at that moment that there would be no longer a relationship with Annette.

It was like that, and sooner or later it had to happen. I was sorry, but then I resigned myself that many things have an end as well as they have a beginning.

My phone rings. It was Angela. He asked me when I returned to Chioggia, he wanted to invite me to spend two days in the mountains.

He needed to be with me for some time. I told her I would be back in a few days, and then I had to go to work.

I was curious about this novelty. Although not very practical and at my first experiences of walking uphill, I would have gladly done it a walk in the mountains.

———

I liked Angela.

It gave me security, I wanted to live experiences among women who opened worlds for me that I did not imagine exploring, like the mountains.

The next morning, I got up early, there was a beautiful sunrise that could be glimpsed between the houses of Nation. I went out, a fresh air touched my face.

I took a walk along the Boulevard de Charonne, which overlooks the Place de Nation. The sky took on more and more intense colors.

The beauty of this city has no equal, in the early morning, then, it is wonderful. I've been walking for a long time; I've come a long way. After the operation not usual to walk I felt good.

I stopped at a flower shop and got some yellow tulips. I always liked them, I thought of Lorenne.

She painted, and she loved tulips. He drew many of them, of all colors. I had to call her, to know how the cure was going, I felt the need, I had a bad feeling. We hadn't heard from each other for many days. I was worried. I had to organize myself to go to Florence too.
I had many things to do, suddenly many commitments overlapped me. It was good for me, I felt alive.

I leave after three days. I get on my train that will take me back to Italy. Full of satisfaction, to have seen my daughter Cecile, my mother and to have spoken with them, to have confided in them.

I looked out the window at that beautiful landscape, expanses of greenery that filled my heart. I was serene, a feeling I hadn't felt in a long time.

I arrive in Milan, I'm about to change trains, I get a phone call. He was Lorenne's companion.

———

"Coraline? I'm Riccardo, Lorenne is not well. He said to warn you and ask you if you can come to Florence. If you want, I organize everything."

It was like a cold shower; chills had gone through my whole body.

I call the company, I communicate the thing, they understand. And immediately I take a train to Florence. It was definitely urgent I had to be there as soon as possible.

I made the journey to Lorenne constantly thinking about the good and bad moments spent together. All our lives there has been something that has bound us.

It is not easy to maintain such a strong friendship at a distance, yet we were capable of it. I was agitated, staring at the people sitting in front of me, but I didn't see them.

My eyes seemed stuck, like my mind. I decide to call Cloe, her voice usually calms me down. It was the first time we spoke directly, our relationship was limited to text and audio messages, some rare video calls, but never a classic phone call of those of the past.

I told her about Lorenne, all our story, it helped me to remember, and she listened with her usual calm, without ever interrupting me. After almost an hour of listening to me, he found the right words, as always, to comfort me, and he also made me smile, telling me some of his tragicomic misadventures.

So without realizing it the loudspeaker
called the stop of S. Maria Novella. I
arrived in Florence and Riccardo had sent
a cousin to pick me up at the station.

The road to their house was short, but to
me it seemed eternal. I did not speak, I
stared at the silhouettes of the hills and the
clouds that seemed to want to chase each
other.

The feeling before entering the house was
frosty, I had thought of a thousand
hypotheses and none was positive, and I
was not mistaken.
Lorenne was sitting there from behind,
looking out of the large window of the
living room overlooking the park. I
approach from behind and embrace her.

She cried, but that was normal for her, her
emotionality was a characteristic that she
had since she was a child, big green eyes,
long black eyelashes, always shiny pupils,
which made that look bright and at the
same time sad.
"What's going on honey?"
She looks at me "You are beautiful"
"Lord what happened?"

"Coraline, sit down honey, we have to
talk"
With broken breath she tells me about the
last few weeks, her illness is wearing her
down, her bones are crumbling, the pains
are getting stronger, she can no longer
walk.

"My future is here, in front of this
window, standing still staring at the world
that revolves around me."
"There is no cure, I will only have to hope
not to suffer too much, I will take drugs
that will make me absent, my life has
stopped"

______

I didn't know what to say, I couldn't even
cry, she got up slowly, with my support.

We went out into his garden and lay down
on the ground, as we did as children, the
sky was getting darker and darker, and
the first stars began to be seen.

Riccardo left us alone all evening, he knew
that Lorenne had many things to tell me,
we talked until late at night then she
collapsed.
In the morning I woke up early, as usual, I
wanted to breathe some fresh air, I went
down, I drank coffee with Riccardo and
then we went out to his property, he
showed me his horses, and all the flowers
and trees that Lorenne had planted.
He was sad, as I was.

All in all it turned out to be better than I
thought, this made it easier for me to leave
Lorenne, I understood that she was in
good hands and that he really loved her.

"Coraline she will die, the doctor spoke to
her, he did not want to tell me anything,
but she knows it, she knows how much
time she has left"
"I beg you not to speak like this, there will
be something that can be done, I do not
accept it, I do not accept it"

When she woke up she took an incredible
amount of medication, we took care of her,
pampered her, and satisfied her.
I spent the whole day with her, then in the
evening I returned to Chioggia with the
last train available.

I came home late at night, I was
exhausted, seeing Lorenne like this made
me lose the sense of things, and of life
itself.

How much suffering he would have to
endure to reach the grand finale.
The next day I started my usual routine
again, my thoughts were fixed on her and
what she could no longer have from fate.

My weight kept falling, the surgery was bearing fruit, I saw myself leaner, and so was it for others.

It was nice to go out in the morning to walk with tight pants and see out of the corner of your eye the guys running around.

A new feeling, which maybe for those who have always been thin is almost annoying, but for me who was obese it was somehow rewarding.

I heard Cloè almost every day, there was always an excuse to make me feel, that girl had something captivating, the desire to know her increased.

There was this opportunity to meet us. I was invited, by a group of mutual aid of which I was a member, to a conference in Rome.

Every opportunity I made the most of to visit Italy and its beautiful cities. So I decided to go, and to propose to Cloe to join me in Rome, since he lived quite close.

I left on Friday night, as soon as I finished work, this time I decided to move with the car, I had finally managed to afford one.

On the way I stopped by Lorenne, I could not stay too long without seeing her, even for just an hour, but it was worth it.

A few weeks had passed since the last time, but her condition was much worse, I stopped only a couple of hours, I did not want to leave her I had a bad feeling, she spoke to me little, her breath was short.
I got back on the road after greeting her with a long hug, in a short time I would have arrived in Rome.
"I didn't think I really came; live you are even more beautiful"
"You also Ciccia" She often called me that. It didn't bother me.

We greeted each other like this in the lobby. We had taken the room on the same hotel. Meeting Cloe was really a dream for me, if you idealize on a person, it often happens that you get hurt when you meet her in person, with her it was not so.

It was night but we went out anyway, Rome has a special charm at night. We slept in the area of Campo dei Fiori, his favorite, two crazy running around the center of the capital, we told each other about everything.

We ended the evening on the Trastevere area in a place overlooking the river. She had everything, she was beautiful, intelligent, very thin, with a strong sense of humor, but above all she knew how to bring out the best in me.

I didn't have the courage to go any further because I didn't want to ruin everything. Back in the hotel exhausted we decided to sleep in the same room, it was very late, we had just closed our eyes, the phone rang, and without even looking at who it was I understood.

"Coraline, tonight Lorenne left, left you an envelope" It was Riccardo, his voice trembled, the pain was felt even miles away. "O my God, I lack breath, how do you feel? Need something?
I leave tomorrow morning at dawn, please try to rest, the last period must have been hard for you, until tomorrow"

I couldn't cry for her, I didn't accept, no one should turn off like this, without having really lived.
I had a feeling of anger mixed with resignation. Cloe hugged me all night being silent, there was nothing to say, being there with her was lucky, no one would have been able to calm me down like she did. My eyes did not want to close, I still had in front of me the image of Lorenne from the back looking out of the window, I did not want to erase it.
I went out at dawn, I said goodbye to Cloè, she would take care of the check-out. "Ciccia, do the good, when you arrive in Florence call me please,"

"He dreamed of high rocks, open spaces and sky above his head. Without it, it was sad"

I have not yet recovered from the loss of Lorenne.

I went back to work, very shaken, he was an important figure in my life. I recognize in her my adolescence, school, the first confidences.

I find myself here facing everything without what was a backbone for me. But I had to react, to think about that point on the horizon that I was struggling to reach.

I will be left with the indelible memories of the moments we lived together. It was time to smile and move on thinking about all the positive things that were happening to me, she would have liked it that way.

I decide to accept Angela's invitation in the mountains. It would have been my first experience after the surgery.

I had promised myself to start a physical activity, to explore new places, I was in a region that lent itself very well to this kind of thing.
She picked me up at home on a Sunday in May.

There was a sun that morning fading from the sea, giving life to a dawn that took your breath away.

We decide to leave to go to a hill not far away.

He had organized an easy route, a sort of small walk on the high ground. She was used to it, but she thought of me at that moment that I was in the early days.

I was motivated, I had to do something for my body, after losing weight, I needed to shape myself by keeping myself in training.

Then I wanted to explore those places I had studied, but only on publications. Now it was time to experience these mountains, and above all to immortalize them. I was also getting passionate about photography.

I had recovered a reflex camera, it was my friend Antonio's, and with that I would have started shooting.
But the best thing was to spend time with Angela. She was sunny, very empathetic, vital.

We spent the whole day on a small promontory, walking among pastures and rocks. I had done my first 10 km uphill, albeit light.

I felt broken but satisfied with what I had managed to do.
Something unimaginable before. Also, this to put in my trunk of experiences that I was filling. The perfect company.

We also ate lying down and on a beautiful lawn. totally overwhelmed and by nature. I was over the moon, yet I had not explored who knows what, I simply breathed that air of freedom.

I had started what would later become one of my favorite pastimes.
"I'll introduce you to a friend who made me fall in love with the mountains. I'm sure you'll like it."

"Angela excites me all this. To think that just last year I could not do even a kilometer in the plains."

At that moment I realized that this was
also a search for feeling good, with the
mind and body everything was part of my
change.

I began to feel like a different person,
more gratified, more beautiful. Yes more
beautiful!

We went out three more, four times.
Always walking. But I was waiting for the
moment to climb to the top.

I had set myself that.
We decide to meet his friend, Marco, on a
Saturday. We would have been out even
at night.

We moved to Trentino, precisely in Val di
Fassa, the goal was to reach Lake
Antermoia.

We meet him along the way, we decide to
leave our car and continue with his. Marco
was a boy of the same age as me, very
nice, smiling, full of life. It was he who
would take me by the hand and urge me
to climb. I was happy and excited.
We do some kilometers and stop to pick
up a girl, Ursula.
I had already known her. Smiling too,
very volcanic, energetic. She sat next to
me, she was tiny and full of spirit.

We talked a lot until we finally arrived at
our destination.

Ursula, despite this somewhat singular
name, I liked her, she gave me confidence.
Angela who was happy to see that we
were so close-knit was proud to have
made me meet her friends.

A few days earlier I had gone to a
specialized shop for the mountain and I
had equipped myself as I could.

I didn't want to arrive unprepared. Ursula
was very complete, she also had a nice
park of cameras.

She was passionate about photography, so
she always found time to escape from
everyday life and launch herself to explore
new places.
I was probably a fish out of water, but I
felt I could do it.

After many hours of walking in the middle of unspoiled nature, we arrive at the Lake.

The scenery is one of the most beautiful that my eyes have ever seen, a true gift from nature.
The transparent water with a seabed of light sand made this lake spectacular, all around a set of mountains of disarming beauty, it was the Catinaccio Massif.

Ursula already knew the place well, so together with Marco they were authentic guides.

Ursula and I took a lot of pictures of each other, the day was sunny, with a few clouds here and there that made the shots even more beautiful. There was immediately a strong bond between us, the passions in common were many, but the most powerful was undoubtedly the desire for freedom, the desire to fly high with our own wings.

A love with her was born immediately, thanks to our passions, our travels, our photos, we had a lot of fun in the following outings, she and I alone, discovering the world. The exploratory tarantulas.

I remember that time when we climbed to the Bell Tower of Val Montanaia, in Friuli-Venezia Giulia.

We left on a Saturday afternoon to go up and see the sunset.

A very difficult task for me, she climbed
like an ibex. We arrived just to see the
fiery sky, and crossed all the shades from
orange to purple, and then leave room for
an incredible starry.

We spent the night up there, alone insoles
on a bivouac of other times, with some
little mouse doing the honors. At dawn we
were already outside, me with my
machine and her with all her complete
equipment, just like a professional.

The descent on Sunday was teeming with
chatter and laughter, as always.
How many photos, the beauty of us is that
we never get tired, we have that duration
out of the ordinary, so no one is behind us,
she has transmitted to me her volcanism
and I my perseverance.

We have promised ourselves that we will chase our dreams together, as much as possible, and one at a time we are fulfilling them.

So on the one hand there is the organization of what you want to achieve, on the other the construction of new dreams, because one thing is certain, neither of them wants to stop dreaming.

"When you think you're no longer able to recognize a place, it's because you're the one who has changed places."

It's 10 p.m. It's hot outside, I'm coming back from work. I was late, we had to deliver a project by tonight.

I did not have dinner, I kept a half sandwich with a drizzle of ham to consume it now. I am with the car of a colleague of mine, mine has given forfait, tomorrow morning I will pick her up and together we will return to work.

There is a beautiful moon. I stop on a very dark spot, I go out to breathe, I take off my jacket, I stay in my shirt.

I want to savor those warm moments before the humidity of the night arrives, which around here is very annoying.

I sit on the sidewalk, discard the
remaining piece of sandwich and bite into
two bites and then take it out with a few
bites.

I was hungry. I ate fast, a habit that I had
stopped since I had surgery. My gaze was
turned to the sky, starry as never before.
I stopped to think. To look if I found
Lorenne's face. That beautiful face that
disappeared into thin air, that left me.

I think about the beautiful things we have
done and how she could abandon me. I
still haven't been able to cry.

Run Lorenne to your new world, do it
lightly, as when we were little we ran
down from the expanses of red poppies.

My life spent between the quarrels of my
parents, between the disappearance of my
father or rather the abandonment. My
mother with the habit of alcohol. A
husband, Jean, arrived perhaps at the most
propitious moment, but not a true love,
the one I was looking for.

I discovered love with the birth of Cecile.
The detachment from her for the search
for my new cage, this time open, which
allows my heart to be able to fly and look
for what it has always wanted.

A different body, more beautiful, more
harmonious. But above all mine. The body
I wanted. How much strength I have
found in doing all these things. An
unexpected, unimagined force.
Were they dreams? What have they been
realized? Maybe yes.

These were my thoughts before
understanding what the meeting with
Annette, then with Maximilian, meant for
me.

Making love to him, after dreaming of it.
With the knowledge that I would have
nothing left. Because it was something else
that I was looking for, what I wanted.

The mountain, Angela who started me
towards this beautiful adventure. His
beautiful friendship, a pure, genuine
person, who just wanted to give me his
good, making me discover what nature
could offer while I was changing.

And then Ursula with her irrepressible
vitality. I think his was a great affection
for me.

If we add Cloè then the circle tends to
close in beauty. The discovery of a female
physical attraction.

I put everything in a big pot that I imagine, that evening, in front of me on the street.

I arrange all these human elements as if I had to prepare a succulent dish that would have gratified my palate.

This was what I thought, retracing the various stages of my life. The one that had led me here, with the people, important and not, that I had met on my way.

And I felt good because they were pieces that had composed and closed my castle. At least I believed this. There was a missing piece.

The most important piece, the one that would make me a happy and fulfilled woman. It was that piece I had to look for. And I would have succeeded, as I did by looking for the other pieces I found.

That castle was beautiful, but something was missing around the corner.

Coraline, I told myself, now it's your turn.
Make this heart fly, blow it up, he knows
where he wants to go. And he will do it
with great lightness because he has
suffered so much heaviness.

He was suffocated by a weight that was
like a boulder, a hermetically locked
padlock.

The heart needs to fly, to expand, to
breathe. Such a heart must be tamed. I
have always suffered this compulsion.
And I think my weight gain is due to this
overwhelming force. Now I am free, free
to love, my body, my soul, the universe.

*"You will stop to rethink the alternatives,
especially after a pain. To everything you have
abandoned to choose something else.
You will have until the end the stupid
certainty that you will always miss something,
except the rare, happy, and precious moments
that you will remember forever, those in which
for no reason you would have wanted to be
elsewhere. Do you know why you will
remember them forever? Because this is love.
In the end, in half a million choices and
renunciations, everything comes down to those
few fragile but pure things that we are not
willing to lose. The rest is finished before we
start."*

I thought this, reflecting on what had
happened to me. You are there waiting
for me, my dear light love. I will find you I
feel close to you. I will never be able to
return to the exact point where I started.
Because I can't find it anymore, I'm no
longer who I was, evolution is taking
place.

I got up, got back in the car and went
home. That night I slept a lot and well. I
also think I dreamed of you, with all the
lightness that was in the air.
Where are you?

*"Love is a constant sum of small
attentions"*

"Every woman deserves a man who is her
elastic, who tends to reach her and then
stop to watch her live free.
The maximum point of love is this, I have
always thought so. Every woman deserves
a man to tell her what I am telling you
now: I want you because without you
nothing is enough for me"

Words that chase each other in my mind,
are like a drum that sounds to remind me
how much I am worth, and that I deserve
a man who dedicates himself to me, as I
have dedicated myself to others.

This is my absolute desire.

I'm going to the sea, it's six o'clock, the sun
has just come out, on the edge of this
expanse of blue water.

I stop to get my feet wet, in front of me a
beautiful light.
I feel myself touching behind. I was
convinced that I was alone, I turn around,
there was a man, also barefoot, bent over
the beach. A man older than me, you
could tell from his step, almost meditative.

"Good morning, I didn't want to disturb
her, I crouched down to pick up a heart-
shaped shell. It was right behind her, it
must not have been a coincidence. I think
nothing comes by chance."

Without even introducing ourselves, I
listened to what he told me, about the
heart, and his in particular, I was curious
and fascinated. A moment in which to
reflect on the soul and the power of
feelings.

That man gave me the pleasure of the beauty of simple things. Yet, it was only a shell with that particular shape, there will have been many others scattered.

But he had lingered on the one behind me. He was cute, a polite person.

He held out his hand to me and made me sit on the damp sand, it was just over six o'clock.
He sat by my side and showed me all the facets of that shell. It naturally expressed what the heart feels when it is crossed by emotions.

Even the shell produces emotions, such as hearing the sound of the sea by bringing it closer to the ear.

"What do you hear? Apart from the sound of the sea?"
He rested the shell on my left ear. I heard not only the sound of the sea but also a little voice that said to trust me.

After the separation from Jean, I only trusted myself and some people I couldn't do without.

But at that moment this little voice I heard told me to listen to this man. And I did, albeit for very little.

"If you hear a little voice in addition to the sound of the sea it means that your heart wants to talk to you, it puts you in front of an emotion that you must feel. Do it, with whom you feel like doing it. But do it. The heart needs attention, more than the body. He needs to feel alive, not closed, free."

He looked me in the eye, smiled at me, stroked my cheek slightly. He got up and left.

I sat there, touched by the sea water that came and went. The sun had risen, and I was enjoying it.

"It is my sun, the one that rises and makes
me find the way, my way to love."
That meeting was no coincidence. It even
seemed intimate to me, with a man I
didn't even know.

He had limited himself to telling me those
phrases, to caressing me, with politeness,
with respect. They were very specific
messages.

I must say that in my life no man has
expressed himself like this, with that
sweetness, towards me.
I got up trying to chase him, but he
disappeared in the middle of the trees of
the pine forest. I never saw him again.

I thought of him all the time as I walked
home. To speak of the heart for me also
meant to speak of love.
I had to be able to free mine.

I wanted to see him again, I didn't know anything about him, not just the name, not even where he lived. I had thought he had a house near the sea. But how could I be sure?
I felt attracted to him. Was it what I was looking for? What did I want? I will never know.
I only have the certainty of what he told me in a few, very few words.

I had to wait for him, as a woman who waits for her man returning from a deep-sea fishing does. By the sea, where we met.

I thought intensely about this image. Wait and scrutinize the sea trying to see beyond the horizon.

What a great feeling I've been feeling since I revolutionized my life. I am proud of myself, of having managed to achieve goals and satisfactions.

I wanted this kind of lightness. And I knew it would come from the sea, I felt it.

I went back there other times, to that precise point, hoping to see him again. But nothing.

I didn't talk about it with anyone, neither with Ursula nor with Angela. I didn't want this episode to be misinterpreted.

I also dreamed of it, but it was not the dream that happened to me with Massimiliano. I didn't want this man to have a sex encounter.

I was impressed by his words and that caress on my face that caused me chills.

I spent my days at work a little sad. And my colleagues noticed it. They asked me what I had, but I replied that everything was fine.

Something told me that I would meet him.
I would have scoured the entire coast to
find it.

I was queuing at the supermarket on a
Saturday morning. There were a lot of
people, and I was getting annoyed.

I turned around to see if other cash
registers had fewer customers to pay.

Distant from me four stations further on I
saw him, with a small shopping bag that
lined up. I stared at him, he hadn't seen
me yet.

He turned around and looked at me
smiling. I smiled at him too, raising my
hand to greet him. He paid and went out.
Once again, I missed the opportunity to
talk to him.

I hurriedly put the groceries in my bags,
walked out to my car, opened the trunk,
put the envelopes in the car and felt his
hand on my shoulder.
"Hello. How are you? There are no heart
forms today" smiling "but I'm glad I saw
you again. I looked for you at the sea but
you weren't there."
So he had also looked for me.
But why do these things when it would
have been enough to show up, exchange
numbers and meet?
This is where the beauty of the situation
lies. It was this chase that made this
relationship more interesting.

"Can we have a coffee?"
"You're sure, gladly. anyway I'm
Coraline"

"Good name, French guess. It can also be
seen from the face"

We went to a nearby bar, very crowded.
We sat opposite each other at a corner.
We had a coffee and talked; he hadn't told
me his name yet.

He was about ten years older than me, he
worked for an airline, he resided near
Venice, near the airport, in an apartment
granted by his company.

He was a person who knew a lot about
life, I realized it immediately. From how
he spoke and the topics he dealt with.
I was a little afraid to talk about myself.

I was very shy, lowering my head while I
had to tell him something.
It had never happened to me before. But I
followed him with so much interest.

He was very kind, very delicate as he told
about himself.

I think I'm very, very attracted to him.
From his way of doing.

It was not the same thing lived with
Maximilian or with other sporadic men. I
also met other people online, much
smaller than me, with whom I had
relationships. That was something else.

I didn't ask him his name, I was waiting
for him to show up.
We stayed for about an hour at the bar. He
got up and held out his hand and helped
me get out of the club. Like a true
gentleman.
Kindnesses that make me feel good, really.
This is called respect, and I was falling in
love with those little attentions. Maybe it
was what I was looking for at the bottom,
then everything else would perhaps come.

We said goodbye, he had to run away to
work, he had a company meeting.
He gave me his phone number promising
to see us again shortly. And I <<when do
we see each other? Soon I hope! >>

In that statement I saw in me a desire to see him again a minute later.
I was glad that we had met, even if by pure chance, especially because he had looked for me.
I think he had a soft spot for me.
I chased him this time in time "Sorry, but what's your name?"
"Pietro, my name is Pietro. Pleasure"
Now I also knew his name, and I was happy. Something was turning from curiosity to interest.
I was fine with him, I felt respected. He wasn't the kind of man who just wanted to take me to bed. I felt desired, cared for.
For a woman it is important to feel protected, even with just words. I felt that way.

He, before running away.

I want to find time for you, to tell you "See you tomorrow". Saying "See you tomorrow" is already a feeling. Because if today I talk to you about tomorrow it means that tomorrow I will be there. "To tomorrow" is a promise, tomorrow is to be there, tomorrow is presence. Tomorrow is that truce of serenity between the past and what will come. Because tomorrow you and I will still be us.

And here I was petrified. Unarmed. No one had ever said those words to me.

They had enormous significance. Maybe I savored something I felt inside, a lightness sought. That way of doing things was very light and at the same time disruptive for me.

I thought well of taking it from the airport when it detached. I saw him a little awkward. In the car he didn't talk much. Who knows what he was thinking.

We went to Venice, along the way he gave
me great advice, he told me about things,
about travels, I was serene, I felt at ease.

It was a fairly cold evening, and there was
a lot of fog. He had never seen that city in
fog. She was as charming as ever.

We walked a lot, we stopped to have a
drink something warm. We laughed, and
we hugged. Hugs that I felt in my skin.

That night I had knocked down all those
barriers that kept me away from him,
either out of shyness, or out of a sense of
inability to let go or out of embarrassment.

He was always correct, honest and
genuine. His integrity gave me a sense of
belonging that I never imagined I would
feel.

It was late, and neither of us wanted to go
home, we were too comfortable together.
We looked at each other and kissed.
Intensely.

I was very embarrassed, but I wanted to
do it, I was the one who took the initiative.
He was happy, at times I even saw him
excited like a child. He felt he had me
inside him.

I was not in love with him, but surely a
very strong bond was being born that
would have led to who knows what.

In another context we would also have
made love. But he was very respectful,
and he didn't make any progress. He
waited for me, looked at me, watched me
and acted accordingly, without hurting.

That night I thought a lot, he had fallen in
love with me, it was clear, I read it in his
eyes always shiny.
Her sensitivity made me a lucky woman.
I had in front of me a man who would
take me by the hand and lead me to my
way.

We went home, I accompanied him, there
was another kiss.

"I'll tell you something. It is not necessary to walk with your eyes down so as not to cross love, but it is enough to lose it.
I will always give precedence to the heart over the mind.
It is the inevitable ordeal of the pure and cursed together. But I learned to live with it. You will laugh at me because I will not have what I want, I will not laugh at you because you do not know what you want. I now find myself and recognize myself. I do it through you, knowing you, living you. I now have myself. You will understand if you have me, if you want me or if you want a refined, complete, unparalleled love. You can find it in me in my soul.
Think about this. Your heart will now speak to you, tell you what it feels.
Mine already knows this."
He left me like that, with those phrases. It belonged to me at that moment, I felt it was mine.

We saw each other times, to walk, visit places. Spending days together, we had a good time.

———

One morning we were by the sea, I lay on
the rocks, I wanted to be kissed.

He gently rested on me and touching me
gave me a long kiss.

I wanted to make love, but in that instant,
I realized that he was stuck, he did not
want to continue, he was not yet
convinced of what I was feeling.
He was in love with me. He could not do
without it.

I was waiting for him, I was always
waiting for a phone call, for a nod.

I don't know if I can talk about love, I
think it was a strong bond, tense between
two people who can't do without each
other. This was light love for me. Looking
for each other, finding each other,
pampering each other. All with lightness
and absolute freedom.

"Mother hello. I want to tell you right
away that I think I have found my soul.
That light love to which I aspired. I
succeeded. I'm not in love with him yet,
but I know for sure that I can't do without
him.
I'll tell you. A big kiss to Cecìle. I go, I
have a heart to follow. "

*I love you with the lightness of a feather that
rests on your breasts. I love you Coraline, my
heart is full of you.*

He wrote it to me with the biro on one
hand. That's who he was.

But I wasn't ready to reciprocate, I don't
even know if I would ever be.

But certainly, it was always a form of love
mine.
How it would go I would find out later.

Meanwhile, I continue to live lightly in everything I do. He taught me to speak with my heart and this is what I welcomed.

"Pietro, I need you, I can't do it alone"
"What is their treasure?"
"Let's envelope open"

Thanks

This novel wanted to be a personal writing, but I feel I can thank for the writing, for the ideas and ideas I had, all my dearest friends near and far and the Cugi. For the composition of the cover, I thank Alex.

I would also like to mention my children Emma Alberto and Nicola, my teachers of life. As well as my family always by my side.

I would like to thank Lorena who if she were here would be proud of me.

I would never have believed to write a book, not even with four hands, I thank Eligio for this opportunity for personal growth, for his patience and devotion in guiding me.

I, Eligio, want to thank you, Maddalena, who with her talent gave me the push to help her express what she had in mind. And he did it very well.